DEBBIE JOHNSON

After spending many years working as a journalist, I decided to stop telling other people's stories, and start making up my own! I work from home in a very messy house near the beach, and write in between pouring bowls of Coco Pops for my three children and my dog (only kidding – he prefers Frosties!). I'm married to a man who is both a librarian and a musician – the perfect combination – and love to write pure, escapist fun. As well as romance, I'm also a published author in fantasy, and am working hard on crime as well. Or writing about it, at least.

Follow me on Twitter @debbiemjohnson.

Cold Feet at Christmas

DEBBIE JOHNSON

Harper*Impulse* an imprint of
HarperCollins*Publishers* Ltd
77–85 Fulham Palace Road
Hammersmith, London W6 8JB

www.harpercollins.co.uk

A Paperback Original 2014

First published in Great Britain in ebook format by Harper*Impulse* 2014

A catalogue record for this book is
available from the British Library

ISBN: 9780008118761

Automatically produced by Atomik ePublisher from Easypress

For Jane and Mark – who renewed my faith in happy endings!

Chapter 1

Jimmy Choo's finest. Pleated white satin. Four inch heels. £500 a pop. For that, you'd expect them to be waterproof, thought Leah Harvey. Or at least to come with jet packs so she could fly out of this godforsaken frozen wasteland, and off to the nearest hotel. Ideally one with a spa, hot and cold running chocolate and Greek god waiters who hand-feed you peeled grapes.

Instead, she was here. In the snow. On Christmas Eve. In the middle of Scottish countryside so remote even the bloody sheep looked like they'd need a sat nav to find their way home.

The lights on the dashboard flickered on and off, casting a final ghostly neon glow before fading into nothingness. She turned the key in the lifeless ignition for the fifteenth time; held her frozen hands in front of the now defunct heating vents, and swore. Long, loud, and with such creative use of foul language that eventually she honked the horn to drown herself out. A self-imposed bleep machine to hide the fact she could make a flotilla of sailors blush.

She undid her seatbelt, noticed that the elegant satin of her ivory dress was now crushed and creased beyond redemption. Not that it mattered. It's not like she'd be using that particular piece of haute couture again.

Climbing out of the cocoon of the car, her feet immediately sank ten inches into freezing cold snow. Her bare shoulders shook with cold, and her fingers and toes decided they weren't even connected to her body as the chill factor took hold. More swearing. This time without the bleep machine. Nearby foxes were probably holding their paws over their cubs' ears.

Great, she thought, turning round to kick the broken-down piece-of-crap car that belonged to her cheating bastard husband-to-be, scuffing the Jimmy Choos in the process. Just great. The perfect end to a perfect day. A gust of icy wind howled up the skirt of her dress, frost nipping at places it had no right to be. Not on the first date, at least. She should be wearing bearskin in weather like this, not a skimpy stretch of silk masquerading as underwear.

She had two choices, Leah decided, teeth chattering loud enough to turn her into a one-woman percussion section. Option One: stay in the car. Wait for help that might never come, as nobody had a clue where she was. Including her. Freeze overnight, and potentially get pecked to death by starving crows she'd be too weak to fight off. The only things left of her would be satin stilettos and her engagement ring.

Option Two: do a Captain Oates and head off across the field to the light she could just about see in the distance. A light must mean habitation, which must mean a human being. Possibly a psychopathic serial killer, or maybe a sex-starved sheep farmer planning Christmas dinner with his collection of blow-up dolls, which, she decided, hitching up the soggy hem of her gown, was still preferable to the crows-pecking-out-eyeballs scenario. She headed for the light.

As she trudged through the fields of snow, she conjured up a playlist of Christmas songs in her head to try and cheer herself up. Or at least help her resist the urge to simply lie down in the ice and sleep. Feed the World. Santa Claus is Coming to Town. Chestnuts Roasting On an Open Fire. Merry Christmas, Everyone... Yeah, right, she thought, slinging her bag over her shoulder and continuing the slow, painful trek to her saviour.

A saviour who probably had one eye, a large collection of shotguns, and slept with his teeth in a jar.

∗∗∗

Roberto Cavelli had just finished reading a letter from his mother when the knock came at the door.

The contents of the letter didn't surprise him – mommy dearest urging him to move on, remarry and give her the grandchildren she so richly deserved. She'd been telling him the same thing for the last two years, and he'd come no closer to settling down. Plenty to bed, none to wed; which suited him fine. But this time she played all her guilt cards: she was getting older, she'd been so ill, she didn't know if she'd even be here by next Christmas... As *if*, he thought, smiling. Dorothea Cavelli was about as ill as a prize-winning ox in the prime of its life. And she was equally full of bull.

Find a wife, she kept telling him. Pretty much every day, but with special intensity at Christmas, Easter and, her personal favourite, his birthday – because, quote, 'you're not getting any younger, darling'. Since when had 34 been declared officially old? Had there been some kind of United Nations ruling that he'd missed out on? Would he be euthanised at 35 if he hadn't started to procreate? And how come the fact that his twin brother Marco was still playing the field seemed okay with her? He was only an hour younger, for Christ's sake. How come he got a pass on the next-generation nagging?

Well, he didn't want a new wife, thank you very much. He still missed the old one. And even if he *did*, even if he admitted he was starting to feel the slow spread of loneliness creeping across his heart like a silken cobweb, it wasn't that easy. You couldn't just go and buy one from Wives R Us. Well, you probably could, but that wasn't the kind of marriage he'd ever be interested in.

Rob knew that not everyone found love behind every door; and not everyone found their soul mate... definitely not twice. He'd had it once, and he'd let it slip away. Some people just weren't meant to have it, simple as that. And some people – like him – simply didn't deserve it. He'd got used to the idea, learned to function alone, to fake a contentment that he didn't feel. It was over for him. He understood that, and accepted it as part of his fate. His mother, apparently, hadn't. She always had been a stubborn old coot.

So while the letter didn't surprise him – in fact it was depressingly predictable, the way she chased him all over the world to give him a ticking off - the hammering on the door did. He stayed at this cottage for the same two weeks every year. Hiding away for Christmas. Giving himself the greatest gift of all – time away from the sympathetic eyes of his family; from the work that dominated his life; from the ghosts of Christmas past. And during all that time, he'd never once heard a single knock. No visitors, no neighbours, no TV – exactly the way he liked it. Just him, several bottles of very good whiskey, and a suitcase full of books. In fact, when he'd first heard the noise, he'd assumed it was another snowfall – waves of the stuff had been thudding off the roof all night.

When he realised it was actually someone banging on the door to the cottage, he instinctively glanced at his watch. After 11pm. Practically the witching hour out here in the Aberdeenshire wilderness. Man, woman and beast would all be tucked up in bed. Who on earth would be traipsing around in the snow on Christmas Eve? Nobody in their right minds, that's for sure, he thought, walking cautiously towards the door.

Maybe, he thought, as he moved away from the comfort of his spot in front of the fire, it was Santa. With an army of marauding elves. They must have heard about the 50-year-old Glenfiddich he was hiding and formed a raiding party.

Well, he wouldn't go down without a fight. Even to a fat man in a red suit.

***

Please God; please Santa; please Buddha... Please anyone out there who's listening – let there be someone in, prayed Leah. And let them open the bloody door. I don't care if they're evil or have two heads or want to slice me up and eat me with a nice bottle of Chianti. As long as they let me get warm first, I'll go willingly. Anything for a hot drink and a pair of bloody bed socks.

It had taken almost twenty minutes to stagger there, and she knew she was in serious trouble. She couldn't feel anything other than pain: stabbing fingers of cold, all through her body, like daggers of ice. Not just going-clubbing-without-a-jacket cold, but proper this-could-be-your-last-Christmas cold. Real, genuine, get-her-a-tin-foil-blanket-or-she'll-die-of-hypothermia cold. The kind you just never encountered in the city, where there was always a McDonald's to nip into, or a bus shelter full of drunks willing to share their body heat. This was different. And if she'd been capable of thinking straight, she'd have been terrified.

If there was no one in – if the cottage was abandoned, with lights left on to scare off the admittedly unlikely burglars – she was done for. The soul-destroying walk would have been for nothing, and the crows would get her after all. The bastards.

The door finally swung open. She felt tears of relief spring to her eyes, then freeze immediately on her mascara-clumped lashes. She looked up, saw the orange glow of a hissing log fire inside; felt the spill of its light and warmth spreading toward her. Even that tiny lick of heat was enough to make her skin tingle with hope.

Standing right in front of her, silhouetted in the flickering shade and wavering shadows cast by the blaze, was God. Or at least it looked that way to Leah. Surely this creature was too divine to be a mere mortal? Well over six foot; midnight black hair; chocolate drop eyes, a strong jaw just the right side of stubble, wearing a thick cable knit sweater and carrying a glass of whiskey. He certainly looked Almighty enough for her right now.

"Hallelujah..." she muttered, and collapsed into his arms.

The last thing Rob expected to see when he opened the door was a woman. No, not just a woman – a bride. A very, very beautiful one at that. Even shaking in her stupidly inappropriate heels she barely scraped five three, but what she lacked in height she made up for in curves. Curves he could clearly see under the satin dress that was soaked onto her like paint; curves that were currently covered in goosebumps; curves that were in fact starting to turn blue. Blonde hair, piled up on her head in a tiara, trailing around her face in tendrils; huge eyes gazing up at him like he was the second coming. Lord, those eyes. The colour of the whiskey in his glass. Pure amber. Lashes tipped by ice flakes; lips parted and shaking as she stared. The Snow Queen looking for her groom.

How on earth had his mother managed this? She was a resourceful woman, but surely even she hadn't been able to deliver a wife for Christmas?

Before he had time to pull a sentence together, the blue-tinged bride on his doorstep muttered one word – he wasn't sure, but it might have been 'Hallelujah' – and fell forward against him. The whiskey glass was knocked from his hand, splashing him with wildly expensive booze and smashing to the floor.

He scooped the woman up into his arms and carried her inside, using one foot to kick the door shut against the howling wind and gusts of icy sleet trying to get in and join the party.

He gently laid her down on the sofa, stroking the melting snow from her cheekbones. She was so pretty…And so cold. Tearing his eyes away from the ample breasts that were now almost peeking out of the strapless satin sheath she was wearing, he grabbed one of the crocheted woollen blankets that were draped on the backs of the furniture, and covered her up. She was in danger of hypothermia. And he was in danger of developing a self-worth problem if he carried on letting his eyes go where they had no right to be. This was not an appropriate time for his libido to come out and play.

He rubbed her hands, leaned over her. Heat. She needed heat. The fire was roaring. The blanket was warm. And he was feeling surprisingly hot himself. Her fingers were like icicles in his grasp, and the breath coming from her lips was still so cold it was clouding into steamy gusts in the air. He edged closer – inches from her face, searching for any kind of response. Suddenly, her lids snapped open, and those amber eyes latched onto his.

He expected to see shock. Fear. Anxiety.

Instead, she murmured 'thank you baby Jesus, Amen'. Kissed him full on the lips. And promptly passed out.

Chapter 2

"Am I dead?" Leah asked almost 16 hours later, when she finally swam back to consciousness.

She'd woken when God walked into the room. He was dressed in faded Levis and a black jersey T-shirt that clung to the muscles of his arms and torso like liquid. He looked suitably celestial, and to top it off was carrying a mug of hot chocolate. With squirty cream on top. For some reason, the words 'squirty cream' and 'torso' blended into one in Leah's brain, resulting in images that were far too vivid to be about God. Positively blasphemous, in fact. If this was Heaven, it had been worth all those years of Sunday school...

She was cocooned in a million tog duvet, her body – naked, which she didn't want to ponder too closely - stretching and writhing beneath the warm fabric, luxuriating in the sensation of soft, cosy heat. Her hair was dry; her fingers had regained a full range of movement, and she could even feel her long-lost toes again. As if that wasn't enough, here he was – her saviour. Sex on a stick and bearing sinful hot beverages. She squeezed her eyes shut, gave her head a shake: Heaven. Must be. The last two days had certainly been enough like purgatory.

"I certainly hope you're not dead," he answered, perching on the side of the bed, long thighs stretching on forever. "Or I wasted a heck of a lot of good whiskey in this mug."

"You're American. I never thought God would be American..." Leah muttered, struggling to sit up straight then realising she had no clothes on and wriggling back down.

"I am," he replied. "American that is. Not God. Although some would say I had delusions of grandeur on that front as well. Glad to see you're feeling well enough to talk. All you did last night and the best part of today was sleep, and sometimes shout about the Hollandaise sauce curdling. Very mysterious. Would it be too much to ask a few questions? Like who you are? And how you ended up here? It's Christmas Day. In the middle of nowhere. And you were definitely dressed for a very different kind of occasion..."

As he finished speaking, Rob saw her eyes flicker over to the hard-backed chair in the corner of the bedroom, take in the fact that her wedding dress, panties, stockings and suspenders were draped over it. He steeled himself for some kind of female hysteria. Because even he – a dumb male of the species — could tell that outfit had presumably been expected to accompany the best day of her life, not one where she nearly died and woke up in a stranger's bed. Buck naked. He'd been trying very hard not to focus on that bit, but as soon as he thought of the words, he felt a familiar twitch in his groin that he knew could embarrass him anytime soon. Should've brought a copy of the paper in with him, ideally a broadsheet.

Leah was quiet for a moment, a small frown marring the milky skin of her forehead as she pieced together the parts of the puzzle. He expected only one possible conclusion: tears, screaming, and possibly physical violence.

Roberto Cavelli took a deep breath in, coiling his muscles ready to run for cover if needed. There was a time to fight, and a time to hide in the broom cupboard, and a wise man knows the difference. Over-emotional women had him sitting on the sweeper every time. He'd leave the cocoa, and run for his life.

Instead, she looked back at him, and smiled. Just like that. A big, gorgeous, open-hearted smile. No shouting. No screaming.

9

No tears. Not even a quivering lower lip. He exhaled, letting out the breath he didn't know he'd been holding. Wow. Maybe she really was from Santa...

"My name's Leah Harvey," she said, sticking her hand out to shake. She kept the rest of her body covered up, managing to awkwardly extend one warm, soft-skinned arm and still look cute. He took her hand in his. It was rude to refuse a handshake, and the Cavelli boys had been raised right.

With the first touch of those soft fingers, he knew he'd made a mistake. He shouldn't be touching this woman at all, even in a hazmat suit. Not with her all warm and curvy, and nude, under those covers. And him with a rapidly developing Crotch Crisis of the first degree. He was going to come across as an utter pervert, damn it.

As her hand clung to his, a tiny spark shot right up his wrist, crawling under his skin like electricity. She felt it too. He could tell by the way she jumped at the sensation. It made the bits of her showing above the duvet jiggle around in a way that did nothing to deter Mr Happy down below. Rob pulled away as quickly as was polite, and crossed his legs.

"Ooh! Did you feel that?" Leah said, giggling and rubbing her wrist. "Must be some kind of weird static thing!"

Yeah. That'd be it, he thought, watching with way too much interest as she manoeuvred herself upright, clutching the sheets in front of her breasts. Her creamy cleavage was mainly hidden by the bedding, but not quite enough to stop a slight spillage of generous flesh over fabric.

Lord, think of something disgusting, he said to himself. Like your brother's sweaty jock strap. Like your 98-year-old Great Aunt Mimi in a bikini. Anything but that killer body in front of you. Not that he hadn't seen it all last night when he'd put her to bed – but that had felt different. That was for medicinal purposes only. He was merely applying correct first aid by stripping her bare of those sodden clothes, that was all. And anyway, he did most of it with the lights off, averting his eyes like a gentleman. None of which had been easy.

"So, what's your name?" she asked, her pink tongue peeking out from between generous lips to lick the cream off the top of her drink. Aunt Mimi, Aunt Mimi, Aunt Mimi.

"Rob," he snapped, sounding a little more terse than he planned. He'd never liked Aunt Mimi. Nasty old coot.

"Okay... Rob. Well, yesterday I was supposed to get married."

"Yeah. My eagle-eyed powers of deduction told me that. Wedding dress and all," he said, nodding towards the now distressed gown hanging limply over the chair back. Leah looked at it and sighed.

"Well, it was supposed to be the whole fairytale deal, you know? Remote Scottish castle. Handsome prince. The only problem was I discovered the handsome prince – Doug — playing hide the sausage with one of the bridesmaids an hour before the service."

"Hide the sausage?" he said, eyebrows raised, slight smile tugging at the corner of his mouth. A mouth, Leah thought, that looked as sinful as his hot beverages. Her eyes lingered on the way his lips curved upwards on one side, like they were asking a question. Wide and full and firm and utterly kissable. Not like Doug's. He had skinny lips. Like his face was so mean it couldn't even spare the flesh. Funny how she'd never noticed that until yesterday. Somehow, seeing him upended in a pile of taffeta had revealed all kinds of little flaws.

"Yes. I'm sure you get the picture. And believe me, he wasn't wearing anything under his kilt either."

"That's... bad. You must be devastated."

Rob stared at her, thinking as he did that she looked the exact opposite of devastated: to him, she looked all silky blonde hair; wide amber eyes, smiling lips. Lips that were now covered in a cream moustache that he'd dearly like to lick off. There was no sign of impending nervous breakdown, which in itself was off-putting. She'd caught her fiancé cheating; abandoned her wedding, and ended up almost dead on his doorstep – yet seemed calm and content. Maybe he should call the paramedics.

"I know," she said. "It is bad. As bad as it gets. And I should be devastated, shouldn't I? I did what any sane woman would – ran away. Grabbed his car keys and legged it. It was only when the bloody thing broke down across that continent of a field last night I realised I might have been a bit hasty. All I have with me is a bag, a phone with no charger, and some make up. Hence my rather bizarre appearance last night. If I'm honest, Rob, which I always try to be, I ran because I realised I just didn't care.

"It should have broken my heart to see his scrawny little backside pumping up and down on top of Becky, but it didn't. I actually felt nothing but relief. It was like something inside me needed to see it, to make me come to my senses. I didn't want to marry him at all. It was more of a wake-up call than a heartbreak. Plus, you know, the whole almost dying of hypothermia thing – it does put things into perspective. I'm alive. I'm warm. I'm drinking hot chocolate and whiskey – very nice, by the way – none of which I expected to be doing last night."

"Perhaps you're in shock," he suggested. "And you'll start your meltdown any minute now."

She raised an eyebrow, seemed to ponder the idea.

"Yes," she replied. "You could well be right. But don't worry – I'll give you some advance notice if I feel it coming on, and you can make sure you're doing something more attractive, like pulling out your own toenails. Right now, though, I feel quite weirdly calm. I'm worrying about the practical things – what happens next. I work with him. For him, really. We share a home, a car. An iTunes account. Everything. And I left it all behind like it was nothing. The only problem was, my great escape—"

"Landed you here. With a man you don't know. On Christmas Day."

"Yep. Oops-a-daisy. I'm sorry if I've intruded; if I've put you out in any way. And I'm really embarrassed I did a swooner on you as well. Damsel in distress and all that – not usually my style.

12

But I was so cold, and you were so warm."

And gorgeous, Leah continued in her mind. And tall. And hunky. Shoulders so wide they filled the doorframe. Legs so long he could probably leap mountains in a single stride. She could have been hallucinating it all last night, but in the warm light of day, he was even better looking: those velvet brown eyes, completely unreadable. That stubble-coated jaw you could strike a match on. Large hands, wrapped around his own mug, fingers oh-so-long. Denim-clad thighs you could so easily see wrapped around you. He was the sexiest man she'd ever seen, and even looking at him was a sensual feast. She could only imagine what touching would be like. His name might be Rob – but she was sticking with God.

And God, she suddenly noticed, was wearing a wedding ring. In fact, he'd put his mug down and was turning the gold band around and around on his finger, twisting it so hard it must have hurt. Ah. He must have been able to read her mind when she was having inappropriate thoughts about him. Or maybe she'd just dribbled. And now, he was sending her a message: back off, taken man.

Received, understood, and undoubtedly for the best, she decided. She was insane to even be thinking of him in that light – right now she should have been starting life as Mrs Anderson, on honeymoon in St Lucia. Instead she was eyeing up tall, dark and gorgeous here, and wondering if he fancied slipping under the duvet for a quick game of tonsil tennis. Maybe she'd taken a bang to the head when she collapsed. Maybe she was experiencing some weird kind of frost-related hormone rush. Maybe she had an undiagnosed multiple personality disorder and would start speaking in fluent Finnish any minute now.

He wasn't even her usual type. Way too big and broad and dark and foreign and sexy. For God's sake, what woman in her right mind would fancy that? She suppressed a giggle, and started to wonder if the concussion angle might be real. She couldn't ever remember having this kind of physical response to a strange man before. In fact, to any man at all. It was completely out of

13

character, but nobody seemed to have told her body that. Her body was convinced that he was its very best friend, and was getting all warm and squishy to prove it.

Even though he was now practically scowling at her, she still had the urge to reach out and touch his jawline, run her fingernails over the stubble and see if it prickled; to trace the bold outline of those lips with her tongue... MARRIED, she shouted at herself. Silently. Even if her body had lost all moral fibre, she wasn't going to start ravishing married men. He could still be a serial killer anyway, even if he did have the looks of a slightly fallen angel.

The way he was looking at her right now, for example, was unsettling. There was quite a lot of Leah on show, she realised, which didn't bother her. She had no problems with body image, and could count her inhibitions on one hand. But his eyes were so dark; his pupils large and black and focused so intensely on hers that she started to feel breathless. Neither of them was speaking, but the air between them seemed to sing, to thrum with some kind of energy. Even the expression on his chiselled face was creating a throbbing pulse between her legs. If someone lit a match, the room would go kaboom, there was so much spark.

"Don't worry about it," he said finally, his voice clipped and short and tense. For a moment she couldn't recall what she'd even said. Oh yes. An apology for disturbing him. Swooning on him. Drooling on him. Fantasising about him.

"There are women's clothes in the wardrobe," he snapped. "I think you'll be way too big for them, though. If you are you'll have to use something of mine."

Right, Leah thought, nodding and smiling as best she could. Thanks a million, mate. That comment definitely slowed the pulse rate down a beat or two: nothing like being called a heifer by an attractive man to kill the mood. She knew she was more voluptuous than was fashionable these days, but she'd never had hang-ups. Men seemed to like it, too. Doug certainly had, until he'd decided he preferred the bridesmaid. But after those marvellously chosen words from Rob, she felt about as feminine as a prop forward for the England rugby team. Too big for women's clothes. Wear something of his. Surely the fool realised that his clothes would swamp her, D-cups notwithstanding? Stupid idiot man.

This particular stupid idiot man seemed to realise he'd said something wrong, as he frowned, glowered, and stood up abruptly. He marched out of the room, absently running his hands through his hair and murmuring something about needing to chop down some trees. He was still muttering as the door slammed shut behind him.

Okay, thought Leah, scampering out of bed and darting through the chilly air to the wardrobe. Weird situation, but deal with it. So he's moody. Probably some eccentric artist type, holed up here in a stone cottage on his own for Christmas. Without his wife... What kind of a wife would let a man like that out of her sight for any length of time anyway?

None of your business, she reminded herself firmly, holding up a pair of jeans that would never in a million years fit her. Surely they were made for a child, not a full-grown woman? No way her hips and bottom would shoehorn themselves into that thimble-full of denim. He must be married to a midget. Okay, that wasn't fair. Speaking as a woman who only topped five foot on a big hair day, Leah knew there was nothing wrong with being vertically challenged.

But this midget must also be really skinny. The kind who made a single pomegranate seed last all day, with one low-fat raisin for pudding. The bitch.

She had better luck with a pair of stretchy leggings, and a plain long-sleeved white T-shirt. Admittedly it looked like it was sprayed on, and there was no bra anywhere near her size. The wedding dress had some kind of industrial strength cantilever device built in, robust enough to support the Forth Bridge, never mind her boobs.

Now she had nothing, unless she wanted to wander round like Miss Haversham all day, in a dirty, torn bridal gown. Yet another genius move on her part. If only she'd known she'd be doing a runner from her own wedding, she'd have packed an overnight bag. She'd kill for her own knickers right now.

She turned and stared into the mirror, examining her ensemble. Oh well, she thought, I am most definitely a beggar, and therefore can't afford to be a chooser. And anyway, you can't *really* see my nipples. Not unless you look really hard. Or they start to misbehave in the cold. She tugged and pulled at her hair, trying to dislodge some of the dried-on product that had moulded it around her tiara, and decided that was as good as it was going to get.

"Hey, Rob?" she shouted as she emerged back into the living area. "Are you still in here? Are you chopping down trees, and if not, can I use your phone? Mine's out of juice and I really need to organise getting out of here."

Getting out of here and getting home as quickly as possible, she decided, was today's mission impossible. Yesterday's had been escape, and later survival. Now she had to move on. To London. To their flat. To get whatever she needed and leave, before she had to face Doug again. To disappear to Timbuktu. Take a midnight train to Georgia. Join a commune in Marrakesh. Become a nun – if they took nuns in when they were 25. Whatever it took to save her dignity and spare them both the useless recriminations. Some relationships simply weren't fixable. Funny how she'd not even admitted to herself it was broken until yesterday. Years of limping along, so used to the problems that they'd become normal. That would hurt at some point, she knew, but not now. Now she needed to be practical.

"There's no signal here," Rob said, emerging from the kitchen, holding a tea towel. He'd obviously decided to dry the dishes before he went logging. He stopped dead in front of her, and stared like she'd grown a third eye.

"What?" she said, feeling alarmed. "What's wrong?"

"That... that top."

"Oh! That. I know. You were right about the clothes. It doesn't really fit, does it?"

"No," he replied, still staring. "You're more..." he trailed off, making vague body-shape gestures in the air with his hands.

"More what?" she asked. Voice quiet. Hands on hips. Eyes narrowed. Oh-oh, Rob thought, recognising that tone. Danger, danger. Tread carefully, lost soul, or you may never pee straight again.

"More... womanly?" he said, looking at her cautiously, one eyebrow raised in a question. She nodded, seemed happy enough with that, thank God. He came here every year for peace and quiet, and he could do without a cat fight with someone he barely knew to bring in the festive season.

Although, he thought, taking another look at that T-shirt and what jiggled beneath, there were some parts of her he was getting to know quite well already. Maybe he'd become immune with repeated exposure, like with flu or chicken pox. Or maybe, a faint stirring in his nether regions told him, not.

"I can see your nipples through that material," he said, dragging his eyes away. "I think that's probably illegal. And if not, it should be."

"Oh," she replied, looking down at her own chest, realising that even his glance had made the nipples in question do some quite embarrassing things. She looked back up, blushing. "I didn't think you could see unless you looked really really hard."

"In case you hadn't noticed, I'm a man," he said. "And it's in our nature to always look at these things really really hard."

Leah laughed out loud, throwing her head back so the creamy skin of her throat was exposed.

Rob, being still male, couldn't help but notice the way the movement made her breasts jut out just a fraction more as she filled her lungs with air and giggled. He wanted to pull that skin-tight T-shirt up, and bury his face in them. Lord, how was he expected to resist her? Should he even try? Where had this sudden attack of morality come from anyway? Must be a Christmas thing. He'd been infected with goodness. Hopefully it was only temporary. He was only flesh and blood, after all.

"I *had* actually noticed you're a man," she said, liquid amber eyes running over his body, taking a lazy inventory of what she saw. Slowly she looked him up and down: legs that seemed as long as her whole body; Levis clinging low to his hips; the curved ridge of pectoral muscles evident through the jersey top. Powerful shoulders, biceps that flexed even as she looked... Gosh, he was an absolute treat. She stared, licked her lips, and filed the image away in her brain. Under S for Sexbomb.

He might be married, but that hadn't made her blind. She couldn't be the only woman who noticed how handsome he was, and anyway, there was no harm in window shopping. Look, but don't touch: the same theory she had for the Stella McCartney shop in Selfridges. Except, in this case, it was harder to resist. She couldn't help wondering if those biceps were as firm as they looked, if that chest was as hard and sculpted as it seemed under the long-sleeved T; how that backside would feel snuggled into the grip of her hands. Whether the tell-tale bulge she could see in his jeans was as promising as the ever-tightening denim suggested. Her eyes lingered low, and she had the suspicion the answer to that one was a resounding 'yes'.

Stop it, Leah Harvey, she told herself. Look at his ring finger instead. Left hand. He's married. To an anorexic dwarf. And anyway, this is not the time for new romance. Or even hot, dirty sex. Your life's in tatters. The man you were about to spend the rest of your years with is a philandering pig. You have no job. No home. No money. And you're supposed to have a broken heart.

Except it wasn't exactly her heart she could feel beating right now. It was something lower, and altogether more primal. She gazed into those dark brown eyes, and had the sense they could stand like that forever, both of them feeling that same beat, both of them frozen in time. They'd be discovered in hundreds of years' time by archaeologist; sexually frustrated mannequins, looking but never touching.

Rob broke eye contact first. He shook his head like a wet dog shedding rain, and murmured something so indistinct it sounded to her like 'Aunt Mimi'. He looked instead out of the window, into the distance. The fields for miles around were white with virgin snow, with more still falling, drifting to the ground like cotton wool buds made of crystal.

"No mobile signal," he repeated. "No landline. No internet. Roads unpassable. And the front door's barely opening, there's been so much snowfall overnight."

"Just you and me then?" she asked.

"Yes. You and me and the snow."

"Right. Have you got a shovel?"

Chapter 3

An hour later she gave up. Each time she shovelled a path clear enough to walk along, more caved in from the sides, covering it in new piles of snow. She was freezing. And wet. And tired. And wondering if Doug had bothered sending out a search party by now. Or whether the guests had eaten the wedding cake and guzzled the bubbly and danced to the mock Motown act without her.

When she first ran out on the wedding party, she'd planned to call him when she got back to the flat. Let him and her friends know she was safe. Family, luckily she supposed, wasn't an issue. She'd hoped to grab the few clothes and belongings she needed and then do a dramatic disappearing act, exit stage left from her old life, and into her vaguely formed new one.

Huh, she thought, that had worked out well. Not. She looked around at the endless, eye-searingly white snow. A woman could go blind out here. And not for any fun reasons.

All things considered, it was depressing. She couldn't even run away properly.

She trudged back into the cottage, kicking off green wellies that were six shoe sizes too big and came up over her knee caps. She could practically feel her nose glowing, and her hair was damp from snow and wasted manual labour. Face it, Leah, she thought – you're just a useless urban gnome trapped in the wilds of the

North Pole. Apparently determined to lose your fingers to frostbite one way or another.

Still, she told herself, pausing to look at Rob sprawled over the sofa in front of the fire. It could have been worse. At least she was a useless urban gnome trapped in the North Pole with God. What her situation lacked in snow ploughs it did make up for in eye candy. Better to focus on the positives than wallow in self-pity, after all. He was reading a book, one arm propping his head up, body stretched so long the T-shirt had crept up over his belly. A few inches of taut, olive-toned skin peeked out. Leah felt her cold nose twitch, like Sabrina the witch, and wondered if she could cast some kind of X-ray-vision spell so she could see the rest of it.

Rob glanced up, gave her a nod of acknowledgement, barely managing to hide the smirk playing around his lips. The bastard. He'd given her the shovel. Told her to knock herself out; that if she managed to dig her way back to civilisation it'd be the greatest escape since Colditz.

Obviously, she'd failed. Maybe she could try faking her papers and digging a tunnel next. She'd probably need to grow a moustache and start wearing an RAF jacket first though.

"Drink?" Rob asked, gesturing to the end of the sofa, where a tumbler of warm whiskey was waiting on a side table. It was practically glowing with deliciousness, and he'd timed it perfectly – just warm enough, as though he'd known exactly when she'd throw in the towel. He was one of *those* people, she realised – the ones who were good at sport and clever and witty and always in charge of the room. Not to mention sexually irresistible to any creature with a pulse. Leah had no doubt that if he'd tried to dig a bloody path, it would be so good it would win the Scottish Path of the Year award.

Rob remained silent, watching as she chewed on her full lower lip, knowing she was weighing up the pleasures of the drink vs telling him to go screw himself. Her hair was scooped into a messy pony tail with an elastic band she'd found in the kitchen. She was wearing his coat, the sleeves rolled over so many times her arms were as big as Popeye's. Peaches and cream skin gone all rosy from the cold, jacket hanging down over her knees, eyes glimmering with chill-sprung tears. Frosty and snowy and perfect; if he could find a way to shrink her, he could hang her from the vast pine tree in the corner of the room as a bauble.

"Okay," she said, hanging up the coat and walking over to the fire. "Move up then. I don't want to have to sit on you."

That, she admitted to herself as he shuffled his legs over slightly, was a big fat lie. She was trying to ignore how big he was, but it was impossible. He was so long, filling the sofa, filling the room. Filling her vision. His hair was messy. The paperback was open, splayed on his broad chest. The truth was she'd very much like to sit on him. Or lie on him. Or curl up in his arms and go to sleep... Those would be mighty fine arms for a woman to curl up in. The fire crackling in the background; the enormous Christmas tree was filling the room with the scent of pine, and there he was. Lying like Adonis on the sofa, asking for trouble. How would he react if she curled up around him like a snoozy kitten?

She raised her glass, and said: "Happy Christmas!", before sipping the whisky.

"Mmmm. This is good," she said. "Glenfiddich?"

"Yeah," he replied, surprised. "How'd you know?"

"I – we – me and Doug. You know, hide-the-sausage Doug. We have a bistro, in London. One of our specialities is fine liquor, as you Yanks might call it. And this is a favourite of mine."

It was also, she knew, bloody expensive. If he was an artist, he was doing well. Definitely not the starving type. Or maybe he'd married money. As soon as the thought pinged into her brain, it came out of her mouth.

"Where's your wife? Why aren't you together for Christmas?" she asked, feeling bolder as the warmth of the whiskey spread in her throat like liquid heat. There were gifts under the tree, and glittery Christmas cards propped up on the bookshelves, which might be from a wife. But there were no photos. No lists of DIY jobs for him to do. No actual woman either – unless he'd killed her, buried her in the woodshed. Nothing but that wide gold band glinting on his finger.

The Dutch courage had helped Leah to ask, and it was a valid question. She'd been feeling some fairly intense heat since she'd fallen into his arms last night, and not all of it came from the fire. She wasn't arrogant, but she knew he'd been feeling it too. He could be as terse as he liked, but she had eyes. She could see what had been going on in those Levis. So far neither of them had acted on it, and it would be better by far if they never did. He was married, and she was heartbroken. Allegedly.

She hoped that talking about the absent missus might defuse the situation, at least for her. This was another woman's man, after all, and she shouldn't be pondering the fineness of his arms, or any other part of him.

"I'm not married," he said quickly, his tone unexpectedly sharp. The mood had been mellow; relaxed. Christmassy, with the fire and the tree and the snow and the whiskey. Now, it was tense. Leah turned her face to his, saw the brooding darkness of his eyes. The gleam of the wedding ring on one long finger. And knew this was not an issue to press. He might as well have pulled out a 'no entry' road sign and stuck it on his frown-creased forehead. She saw the line of his jaw go rigid with anxiety, his body language screaming 'none of your business'. A mystery. And not hers to solve.

"Okay," she said, after a beat. She kept her gaze on the blaze of his eyes, smiled, aimed for a light-hearted tone that might bring him back down from red alert. "Well, me neither, as you know. Lucky us. And you were right, of course. I failed abysmally in my attempts to dig us out. Is it all right if I stay? Is there maybe room in a stable somewhere? I know I arrived in an Audi, not on a donkey, but I don't mind roughing it if you need your space."

"You can stay," he answered, quietly. He was so glad she hadn't asked any more about Meredith. He came here to escape talking about Meredith. His family seemed to think talking about her was the way to 'cure' him; and his sister-in-law Melissa never failed to try and reach out at this time of year, get him to open up. Idiots. Lovable, but idiots all the same. He'd resorted to flying to the other side of the world to avoid them all. The last thing he needed was Leah quizzing him as well. He could feel the attraction between them fizzing so loud he could almost hear it pop, like soda bubbles. That, he could cope with. He might end up with blue balls, but he could cope with it. Deep and meaningful conversations about his past, though? No way.

He shook it off. She'd lightened the tone, and he knew it was for his benefit, that she'd picked up on his signals. She'd mocked herself, pulled such a disgusted face at her path-digging failure that he'd had to smile. She'd backed off. In that one exchange she showed she was more in tune with his feelings than the entire Cavelli clan back home in the Windy City. She already understood and respected the boundaries that they relentlessly tried to demolish every year. They could do this: avoid the deep and meaningful. Hopefully avoid sex. Avoid everything with screw-up potential until he could safely get her out of there.

"You can stay, Leah," he repeated, "but don't get any ideas. I sleep with a rape alarm by my bed, and I'm trained in seven different types of martial art."

She giggled and drained her whiskey. He was betting she'd be ready for a top up, and he knew he was. All of this suppressed lust was thirsty work.

"Damn," she said. "And here was me planning to get you drunk and seduce you. The temperature's dropping you know – we might be forced to strip off and share body heat to survive!"

She was joking. He knew she was joking. But there was something bubbling between them, something so powerful the rest of the room seemed to fade into the background. The radio was on in the kitchen, and choirboys were singing about little drummer

24

boys. The reception was poor, and the sound was crackling. The logs in the fire were crackling. And they were crackling, with raw sexual energy.

Leah looked at him, noticing the quizzical upward twist of his lips, the sideways quirk his mouth took when he was amused or intrigued. It was strange, she thought, how after only a few hours in his company she could already spot his familiar expressions. His eyes, though, they looked completely new. There was a glimmer of golden flecks she'd never noticed before. Like the flames of the fire were somehow leaping around in the chocolate brown of his pupils.

"Only kidding," she added, suddenly feeling a flush of heat rush through her – heat that had nothing to do with the blaze in the fireplace, or the excellent whiskey, and everything to do with the big man lying next to her.

"Do you always talk this much?" he asked simply, locking his hands behind his head and gazing up at her. His eyes skimmed her chest on the way to her face, and her nipples tightened in response. She felt her pulse rate soar and knew she was blushing. Again.

"Only when I'm..." Nervous, she thought. Terrified. Aroused. "...awake," she said.

"Do you remember when you came to, last night? After you fainted so delicately into my arms, smashing whiskey and glass all over the place?"

"Sorry! But, no. Nothing at all. Just getting here, and being so relieved when you opened the door, then waking up this morning. Why? What did I miss?"

"You sat up, praised the Lord, and kissed me."

"Oh! Sorry again! That was very forward of me!" she said, torn between embarrassment and laughter. In the end, laughter won out – surely it wasn't such a big deal? She'd been barely conscious at the time. The ultimate let-out clause. Shame she hadn't had a quick grope of his arse while she was at it, in fact.

"Well, how was it for you, then, this kiss? Obviously not that good for me, given that I don't even remember it."

She gave him a look she knew was way too flirtatious. She was still thinking about his bum, and wishing she *could* remember the way those luscious lips had felt on hers. Where was the harm in a bit of casual flirtation, anyway? After all, as they'd now established, neither of them was married – despite him wearing a ring and her turning up in a wedding dress. Appearances could be deceptive.

He didn't reply, and she wondered if she'd blown it – he was a moody so-and-so, flirty one minute, closed off the next. Or maybe he was just so arrogant he couldn't stand even a joking critique of his snogging skills.

He reached up and grabbed her shoulders, suddenly tugging her down onto his chest. She landed with a thud, and lay there for a second, stunned in several different ways. Oh. Yes. It *was* just as hard as it looked; pure muscle. And he smelled really, really good. Of wood and spice and something that took a direct route from her nostrils to somewhere much lower. Never had the simple act of breathing been such a turn-on. She lay still, inhaling the fresh cotton of his T-shirt, the hint of something gorgeous from the shower, and the underlying scent of him... sexy, virile, male.

She pushed herself up, her face inches from his, taking tiny breaths as she lost her gaze in the pool of those gold-flecked eyes. Deep enough to drown a woman. Even looking at him was divine, and the feel of his hard body crushed under hers was even better.

Rob tangled one hand into her hair, not even knowing himself what he was going to do next. There was something about this woman that confused him, intoxicated him. Took away his ability to think clearly. In the end, without thinking at all, he pulled her mouth down to meet his.

He kissed her softly at first, giving her the chance to pull away – part of him even hoping she would. When it became clear from the way her body moulded to him like running water that she was going nowhere, the contact deepened. Mouths parted, his tongue touched hers, his teeth sweetly nipped her lower lip. One hand held her head firmly to his while the other roamed expertly over the contours of her body – her neck, shoulders, down to the small of her back, caressing and stroking with fingers that clearly knew their way around a woman.

Leah was thinking no more clearly then him. Her body was filling with warmth; a thousand nerve endings tingling as his hands and lips dominated her senses. She could feel his arousal pressing into her, and she slid shamelessly around on top of him, wriggling her body into position until the hard denim-clad bulge hit just the right point to make her gasp. She slipped a hand under his T-shirt, tracing the smooth lines of his pectorals, the silky trail of hair, the peak of his nipples. Jesus. What a body. She wanted to pull that jersey away, to look at him and lick him and kiss him all over.

As fast as it started, it ended. Suddenly, he pulled her face away, using the tangle of her hair to hold her back, ignoring her small pleas and moves to return to his kiss. He looked up at her confused expression with a big, dazzling grin, eyes wicked and teeth gleaming white.

God, she was magnificent, he thought as he gazed at her. Lips swollen from kissing him back so hard. Eyes wild with desire. Her body bucking and rubbing like she was riding a rodeo horse; her fingers already instinctively seeking out the parts of his body that were the most sensitive. Those lush breasts straining to escape. He was so turned on his whole being was thrumming. And still he held her back. He had a point to make, and Rob Cavelli was very good at making his point.

"As the last kiss disappointed you so much, d'you think you'll remember that one?" he said, smiling as her lust-clouded eyes started to clear. The amber settled from tigress to kitten, and she sighed as she realised she'd been played.

"Yes. 'Til I'm 100 and senile," she said breathlessly. "Point taken. But why did you stop? You seemed to be enjoying it as well."

"Of course I was. But you might regret it later," he said, his voice gravel. "Your judgement doesn't exactly seem to be working right now. And because this is how babies are made, and I'm sure neither

27

of wants that for Christmas. And because I'm hungry. For food."

Even as he said it, he knew he was lying. Making excuses. He was nothing but a coward, pretending to protect her, when in reality it was himself he was worried about. Sex with this woman would blow his mind, he already knew it would. And that would be very unsafe sex... in all kinds of ways. He was buying time. Trying to get his body to cool down so his mind could take control. He hadn't lived like a monk since Meredith, but no woman had ever come close to making him feel like this. It was crazy, and he'd already been too crazy. He lived there for a long time after he lost Meredith, and he never wanted to return.

He kept his face closed, guarded, making his expression as light as his tone. Leah smiled at him, and knew he was stalling. Decided, he knew, to go along with it. Good girl.

"Food." she murmured, sitting up so she was straddling him. She tidied her hair back into its pony tail and gazed ahead, deep in thought. From this angle he could see the firm buds of her nipples thrusting proudly forwards, her body still bearing the remnants of her arousal. Even the thought of it made him twitch in the pants department, and he firmed up against her again, so hard there was no hiding it. She wriggled against it, very deliberately, as she pretended to ponder dinner plans.

"Well, if you're sure it's food you're after, I'm your girl. You happen to be in the company of one of the finest chefs in London – or at least on one street in London. I'll go and see what's in the kitchen..." she said, and nimbly climbed off him. He felt cold as soon as she'd gone, already missing the soft press of her body.

She looked down, grinning at the sight of his distressed groin.

"You just lie there and think about what you're missing." she said, and swayed out of the room, rounded butt sashaying in those impossibly snug leggings.

Oh God, he thought. I may never walk again.

***

"This is good," he said, dipping freshly baked bread into home-made French onion soup. "Really good. How did you manage it?"

In just a few hours Leah had filled the cottage with the scents of a home; raiding cupboards, plugging in appliances, and even figuring out how to use the Aga range he'd been using as a butt-warmer for several years now. It had been a great butt-warmer, but he'd never used it to cook.

Leah grinned at him. Few things pleased her more than people enjoying her food, and this particular man enjoying it gave her a bad case of the warm and fuzzies. Even watching him eat was sensual, she thought, the way his face reacted to the flavours, the pure pleasure of the taste.

"It was easy. So easy even you could do it. There are all sorts of great things in your kitchen. Don't you ever use it?"

"Not really," Rob admitted. "I only come here for these two weeks. Morag, who lives here the rest of the time, always leaves stuff for me – but I have to be honest, I tend to exist on tuna pasta and grilled cheese sandwiches for the whole fortnight."

"Grilled cheese! That's so cute!" she said, stifling a laugh as he stared at her. "You mean cheese on toast, Rob. Come on, get it right. You may be an artist, but that's no excuse for not learning the native tongue."

"Artist?" he said, blankly. That was quite a gear shift, and he had no idea what she was talking about. "Who said I was an artist?" he asked, confused, wine glass halfway to his lips. Did he have paint on his sweater, he wondered? Smell of turps? Nothing could be farther from the truth – he was the kind of kid who was still drawing stick figures at 12.

"Erm, nobody did, now you mention it," she said, "that was just my wild brain conjuring things up, I suppose – and once I'd thought it, it became true in my own mind, you know?"

She'd tied her hair back with a piece of tinsel she'd lifted from the pine tree, and it was draping metallic red glitter over her shoulders, merging with the blonde of her messy plait. Very festive, he thought. Morag decorated the tree for him every year, even though he'd told her he didn't care. It was nice that someone was finally appreciating her efforts.

"I think," she continued, narrowing her amber eyes as she tried to reconstruct her thought processes, "it was because I couldn't imagine why else somebody would be holed up here on their own over Christmas, unless they were, I don't know, seeking inspiration or communing with the spirit world. Maybe an artist, or priest on some kind of retreat. Clearly not in your case – at least I hope not, bearing in mind our adventure on the sofa earlier... so I decided artist. I was wrong, obviously. So what *do* you do – and why are you here? You don't have the excuse of it being an accident like I do."

"I'm a white slaver," he answered, his teeth shining savagely in the flickering light cast by the fire. For a second she could believe that, with his olive skin and dark eyes. And he'd look amazing in a pirate costume.

"I wait here for passing virgins," he said, "then I sell them on for unimaginable profit."

"Oh dear. Sorry to let you down on the virgin front. You must have thought your luck was in when a woman in a white dress turned up on your doorstep?" she replied, shaking off the image of Rob and his swinging cutlass. Leah had been nipping at the wine all the time she cooked, and accidentally seemed to have polished off most of a bottle of red on her own. Oops, she thought. This was turning out to be an unexpectedly boozy Christmas Day after all.

"Nah, it happens all the time. I'm forever fighting women off," he said. "Gets quite exhausting after a while."

That, thought Leah, she could definitely believe. This was not a man who would ever go short of offers. From man, woman or beast. He was impossibly good-looking. Italian family, she'd managed to learn. Lived in Chicago. White slaver. That was the sum total of her knowledge about him. Assuming you didn't include the way his lips tasted or having a fair estimate of his penis size, that is.

"No. Really. Go on. Tell me something about yourself. I mean, I've already poured my heart out to you, and you've seen me starkers. It's only fair."

He had seen her 'starkers', he acknowledged. At least when he hadn't been squinting to try and avoid it. And now, thanks to that casual comment, he was imagining her starkers again, wearing just the tinsel in her hair.

"Sorry to disappoint you," he said, shaking away the image, "but I'm not an artist. Or even a white slaver. I'm just a businessman. Family firm. Corporate suits. Meetings all day. Boring to the max."

"I bet it's not boring at all. I can't imagine you doing something boring," she said. "I bet you buy and sell something really interesting, like, reindeers. Right?"

"You guessed it," he said, smiling. "I'm a reindeer wholesaler. And by this time of year, I've had enough, so I run away to the wilds of Scotland to escape it all. And do a bit of stock-taking while I'm here."

Something about the way he said it rang true to Leah. Not the reindeer bit, obviously, she thought, but the escape. The running away. Even the stock-taking. She'd known this man for less than 48 hours and she already realised he was strong; dependable; in charge. Of himself and probably of others. At certain moments already, of her and her newly emerging nymphomaniac. But despite all of that, he also needed to escape. To hide.

What could be bad enough to make a man like this feel the need to hide? Would she ever find out? Too serious, she thought, reaching for yet more wine. Way too serious, and none of her business. They'd been thrown together by a set of freaky circumstances and he'd been kind enough to let her stay, and even to share some saliva with her. She should repay him by keeping her nose – and all of her other body parts – out of his business.

"Well, I understand that," she replied. "I'm a fugitive myself. I ran away into the wilds of Scotland too, away from my own wedding, shortly after seeing Doug disappear up Becky's frock.

Okay, I was aiming for London and I ended up—"

"Here, with me. Which is no sane person's idea of an escape," he said, his tone suddenly quiet and serious, his face cast down in the shimmering firelight. There was a sadness in this man, making guest appearances when Leah least expected it. She felt her own pain well up in response; scrunched up her eyes so she wouldn't cry. What a pair of losers.

It was Christmas, she told herself. And nobody should be allowed to be sad at Christmas — no matter how good the reasons. It is, after all, the season to be jolly.

"Yep. I ended up here, with you, Mr Cavelli. Where I've had to endure sexual harassment, and been forced into becoming your chief cook and bottle washer. Talking of which, are you ready for your next course, sir?"

"Yes. Into the kitchen, woman," he said, noticing the way she'd picked up on his mood, and tried to deflect it. Moving his mental course... what? His usual default setting of morose solitude? Around this time of year it seemed to be the only mood he was capable of. God, he was becoming a pain in the ass, he decided. He was even sick of himself.

Yet with Leah around, he felt different. The anxiety felt diffused by the easy positivity and flirty charm that seemed to be *her* default setting. He knew she must be in pain; knew she must be grieving for her lost future, no matter how much she mocked herself and her circumstances. Nobody could walk away from that kind of experience unharmed. And this Doug guy must be a total idiot. Who could have a woman like Leah waiting for him and still want more?

Not love... but chemistry. Burning, sparkling, blazing chemistry that threatened to set them both on fire. She was way too vulnerable for that right now, even if she didn't think she was. And as for him - he always would be too vulnerable. After Meredith, there was nothing left to give. His body, yes. But more? The sort of more a woman like Leah deserved? No. That part of him just

32

didn't exist any more. And that's what his Mom and his brother could never get. He wasn't choosing to be alone, any more than he'd chosen to have dark hair, or an aptitude for numbers.

It was part of who he was now. Who he was destined to be. There was nothing anyone could do about that – not his mother, not his brother. Not himself. Not even Leah.

Chapter 4

His dark thoughts were scattered as Leah bustled back in from the kitchen, holding a hot plate with the edge of a cloth. The red tinsel had glued itself to the side of her cheek, skin flushed with the heat of the kitchen.

"It's only a steak," she said, sounding nervous and happy and excited all at the same time. "I found it in the freezer. Just a little sauce to go with it, peppercorns; some nutmeg, cream and—"

"Brandy," he added as he took his first bite. "Because we've not had enough booze so far today, right? Leah, it's delicious."

And it was. Simple, luscious and full of flavour. He knew this wasn't a well-stocked gourmet kitchen, despite her claims. Leah had taken the absolute basics and conjured up something wonderful. The woman had talent. And passion – he could tell that from the way she hovered, waiting for his reaction. This was something she loved doing. He wondered, even though it was none of his business, what she'd do with all that passion now, if she couldn't go back to the bistro she'd mentioned.

He looked up and smiled. Leah felt her heart do a little flip for no good reason. She was always cheered when people enjoyed her cooking, and when the satisfied customer came with the face of a Renaissance god, the body of an athlete and the tongue of a sinner. Well, she thought, that was what you called a good tip.

She'd quite like to heat him up with some brandy and cream and serve him as pudding.

She sat down to eat, realising how much she'd miss that first-bite reaction. How much she'd miss the bistro. Scouring the farmers' markets for the freshest produce. Creating new dishes; giving them silly names and chalking them up on the specials board. She's miss the hustle and bustle of restaurant life. The staff she worked with; their regulars, the blokes who ran the bar over the road, the homeless guys she saved leftovers for. She'd miss all of it, so much. It had been her reality for years – nice, fun, safe – and now it was all gone.

Now, though, she reminded herself, was not a time for moping. Reality sucked, and therefore it could wait. If she crashed now, he'd go with her – and they'd spend the rest of Christmas Day sobbing into their wine glasses.

Rob's plate was soon clear. He didn't lick it, but she could tell he wanted to. The ultimate compliment. It lifted her spirits straight away – if she achieved nothing else this Christmas, she'd fed a delicious meal to a delicious man. Even if he wasn't hers for keeps.

"Just wait 'til you taste dessert," she said, raising her eyebrows in an exaggerated leer. Before he could respond, she disappeared off into the kitchen again, carrying off their used plates. She gave her bottom an extra wiggle as she went. Or the red wine did, at least.

Rob smiled as she wiggled her ass at him. He sat still, leaning his elbows on the table. His belly was full of fine food, glass full of fine wine, his mind full of a fine woman... and he needed to ease up on all three. He was enjoying himself way too much. Way more than he deserved.

He could hear Leah singing in the kitchen, murdering one of the carols being broadcast on the radio. Oh Come All Ye Faithful. He shook his head in amazement at her resilience. After seeing their fiancé doing the dirty with someone else, most girls would be snivelling in a corner, desperate to win him back or stab him in the eye with a stiletto heel. Instead, here she was. No sign of a nervous breakdown, or at the very least a firm grip on when she was going to allow it to happen. Distracting herself with cooking and singing and making him laugh. Not to mention kissing and wriggling and touching. God. He was getting hard again, even thinking about that action-packed little body of hers.

As he once again plundered his brain cells for anti-aphrodisiac thoughts, all the lights went out, and the cottage was plunged into total darkness.

Shit, he thought, blinking against the night until his eyes adjusted. The generator must have failed. Again. Happened at least once every year. One of the many joys of rural isolation.

He heard a shriek from the kitchen and the sound of a plate falling to the floor, smashing on the cold stone flags. Rob scraped back his chair, felt his familiar way to the drawers and pulled them open. Once he'd managed to find the candles in their usual place, he dashed through to the kitchen.

"Sorry!" Leah said, voice high and nervy. "I just got a shock when it all went dark! Hope it wasn't priceless porcelain or anything."

She was squatting down in the darkness, trying to pick up the broken shards of pottery; hands shaking, feet bare.

"Shush, it's fine," said Rob, offering a hand to pull her back up. "Leave that until we have light, I don't want you to cut yourself."

She ignored his outstretched hand, and carried on scrabbling for the broken pieces, skimming her hands across the stone to find them.

" Leah. Listen to me, for Christ's sake. Stand up in case you get hurt, there's pieces of plate all over the damn floor and you have nothing on your feet."

"No, no, it's okay. I can't leave a mess like this," she said, her pale skin luminous in the dark, toes missing the sharpened slivers of porcelain by inches as she scooted around the floor. With an exasperated sigh, Rob leaned down, scooped her up into his arms, and deposited her with a small thud on top of the work surface.

"Oh!" she said, perched on the edge of the counter on her

36

bottom, feet waving from side to side because her legs weren't long enough to reach the floor. "You picked me up! And I'm huge!"

"Yep. Just like a baby elephant, but not as cute. Now sit still there while I look for the matches. They're behind you."

Rob leaned past her, his body crushing against hers, as he stretched his arms up to reach a shelf above Leah's head. He could feel the warmth of her breath against his chest, smell the sweet fragrance of her shampoo, and knew that if he looked down into those amber eyes – even for a split second – he'd be lost. All resolve would be gone. And as Leah seemed decidedly tipsy, hers had probably already run for the hills.

"Erm, Rob," she said, the ever-present sound of laughter in her voice, "is that a candle you're holding or are you just pleased to see me?"

He could feel her body shaking against his as she giggled; could see the downright playful expression on her face even without electric lighting. She was asking for trouble and, frankly, he was desperate to give it to her.

He slammed the candle down on the counter. Vision could wait, he decided. There were more pressing senses to be dealt with.

She squeaked slightly as he shoved his way between her dangling legs, took her face in both his hands and held it firmly inches from his. Now he had her – what was he going to do with her?

Leah was wondering exactly the same, and it felt delicious. Even in the darkness she could see the blazing intensity of those gold-brown eyes; the twist of his mouth, the flare of his nostrils. Oops. Maybe that had been one flirt too far, she thought, already swamped by the warmth of his breath on her face; the knowledge that all she had to do was lean in to those luscious lips for a kiss. She knew she shouldn't. She knew she might have had a bit too much to drink. She knew she was in no emotional state to be jumping into bed with someone new. She knew it was Christmas. She leaned.

The heat was immediate as their lips met. Rob's fingers caressed her cheekbones and jaw as he kissed her, then plunged into her hair, pulling it back from her face, holding her steady as the kiss intensified. The feel of his hard-planed body thrusting up against hers was exquisite; he wanted her as much as she wanted him, she could feel it in the urgency of his kiss, the push of his body. She instinctively hooked her legs around his waist and tugged him in tighter, rubbing herself up against him. He made a low growling sound and responded in kind. We're so, so close, she thought, we'd be having sex, if it wasn't for those pesky layers of clothing.

He used the hands tangled in her hair and pulled her head to one side, leaning in to nuzzle the soft skin of her neck. The touch was barely there; a trace of tiny kisses and nibbles under her ears, across her throat, spreading to her shoulders, finding the tiny dips and hollows in her flesh that drove her wild. She'd expected brutal and hard: instead he gave her slow and sensual, and every inch of her body was begging for his mouth.

"Rob, please…"

""For once, be quiet," he muttered. "I'm busy."

He pulled back, lifting his face to hers, their eyes meeting in the glow of the moonlight flooding in through the window.

Never once breaking eye contact, Rob slid his hands beneath her T-shirt, and a shudder ripped through her as he placed them on the bare flesh of her waist. His fingers softly skimmed upwards, inch by slow, torturous inch; all the time the feel of his arousal pressing into her through the flimsy fabric of her leggings. She scooted her bottom forward even more until she was almost resting on him, getting as close as she could and still wanting more.

His breathing was low and jagged as his hands moved upwards. And Leah, she was barely breathing at all, lost in the power of his eyes, the sensation of long fingers stroking their way up her body, over her stomach, her ribs, edging ever nearer to the place she needed them to be. Her nipples had tightened into hard, explosive buds of excitement, and her breasts had taken on a life of their own, pushing themselves forward to meet his searching touch.

Rob stroked the underside, the curve that jutted upwards; the delicate flesh of her areola puckering under his touch. He paused, felt the weight of her breasts in his hands, then captured one desperate nipple between finger and thumb, rolling and rubbing, sending an edge of delicious pain shooting through her body.

Leah tangled her fingers into the midnight of his hair, pulled his lips to hers, drinking in the passion and sensuality of his mouth.

"I need this," she muttered. "Please. Don't think about it. Just do it."

He nodded. Tugged the T-shirt over her head. And thought he might come there and then when he saw those magnificent bosoms in all their glory; full and round and topped with perfect, hard nipples. He leaned forward, lifted one breast, and took the nipple into his mouth, tracing its contours with his tongue before sucking, gently at first, then harder, knowing from her quivering body, the feel of her fingers in his hair, that she was loving it. He moved to the other, all the while her quiet moaning begging him not to stop. As if. He couldn't stop if he wanted to.

He lifted her slightly, pulled the leggings down, moved his hand to her parted thighs. God, the heat was amazing. She was on fire. He glanced at her face: eyes glazed, mouth open, tiny whispers urging him on.

He slid one long finger inside her, was instantly engulfed with moist heat as she started to thrust. He used his thumb to circle the swollen bud of her clitoris, all the time probing her with a steady rhythm her body was matching.

She clung on to him, hands gripping and ungripping the fabric of his T-shirt, hair wild around her face as the pleasure mounted. She realised that she was losing all grip on reality; everything was now dominated by the feel of his fingers on her and in her, on the exquisite edge of sensation that was building up in waves, bigger and nearer and closer and... Oh! Everything exploded. Everything. For what felt like minutes, the orgasm ripped through her body with such ferocity she thought she might black out.

Her face collapsed forward, buried in his chest, as he stroked her hair and kissed her and murmured her name. Eventually she took a deep breath, looked up at him. At this virtual stranger; at this man who'd just shown her everything she thought she knew about sex was wrong. That everything she'd believed to be good in the past was just a pale imitation of what it could be. This was what sex could be, should be, like.

It was a revelation.

Rob's pupils were enormous, and she could still feel his huge erection through his jeans. He'd waited. Held off. Accepted her need, and given her what she wanted. And it must, she thought, sliding from the counter and on to her wobbly legs, be killing him.

She dropped down to her knees, unbuckled his belt and released him. Jesus. What a monster. Hard and happy and ready to go.

"You don't have to—" he started.

"Shush. I want to. I really want to. And I think you," she said, leaning in to run her tongue all the way along his shaft, "want me to as well."

She took him into her mouth, licking and lapping and exploring, finding ways to pleasure him despite his size, her tongue flickering everywhere, her hands stroking and rubbing and building up in a rhythm that was clearly right for him. She reached round, gripped that improbably perfect backside of his, and urged him on even further; lifted her breasts so their soft flesh cushioned him; sucked him until he could take no more. He gasped and shuddered and finally came.

"Jesus, Leah!" he said, pulling her to her feet. "Were you trained in a bloody bordello?"

"Same could be said for you," she replied, wrapping her arms around his waist and snuggling into his chest. "Except, you know, a bordello for boys. Happy Christmas, Rob."

He laughed; he knew they shouldn't have done it, but frankly he didn't care. Sometimes the body wants what the body wants. And the brain can go to hell.

"Happy Christmas, Leah."

She held on to him like she was drowning.

"Sorry," she said, face still crushed against his chest, "but my legs are wobbly. I think I might need a lie down."

"Um. Not a problem," he said, feeling himself hardening again already. Waiting for sanity to return and realising he might be waiting a while; having Leah's bare breasts rubbing up against wasn't exactly a passion-killer.

He held her hand and led her towards the bedroom in the darkness. It was only when she sat down with a small 'ouch' that he realised she'd been limping all along.

"What is it?" he asked, hoping he hadn't done something to unintentionally hurt her. Surely he hadn't... Not yet, at least.

"Plate. In foot. Sorry. Got distracted earlier. Concentrating on other body parts. Probably could've amputated one of my toes and I wouldn't have noticed."

"Idiot," he said affectionately, getting up to fetch the long-forgotten candle, along with a small bowl of warm water and a cloth. It gave him a minute to cool down. In all sorts of ways.

He kneeled down before her, lifting her foot in the candlelight to examine it, gently wiping and stroking until the tiny sliver that was wedged in her flesh came free. As he washed the small wound, face intense in concentration, Leah felt something shift in her heart.

His face was so focused; his touch so soft and tender as he worked, so careful not to hurt her. Minutes earlier he'd been an animal – all heat and need and hard sex. Now he was kind. Kind. Yep. That was the word – and that was what was her undoing. Kindness. She didn't realise how starved of it she'd been until now, she thought, as tears sprung to her eyes. Her and Doug... they'd rubbed along okay. He'd not been cruel, not until their wedding day at least. But they'd not been close either, not cherished each other enough.

Rob looked up. He saw her crying. Saw big, round tears spilling from the corners of her amber eyes, trailing over the peach of her skin and pooling in her neck. He felt a constriction somewhere tender in his chest; in a place he thought he'd shuttered up forever.

"What is it?" he asked. "Am I hurting you?"

"No; no you're not. It's just... It's been a weird couple of days. The wedding. The running away from the wedding. And now this. It's all been quite a lot to take in. "

"Of course it has," he said, keeping his face neutral. If she started sobbing about how much she still loved her ex right now, he wasn't sure his ego could take it. Most women, after kitchen lust with Rob Cavelli, only had eyes for him. Still. There was always a first time.

"It's not *him*," she said, as if reading his mind, wiping her eyes with the back of her hand. "Not Doug. It's everything. The fact I lived with him. That I agreed to marry him, when all the time, I never even really loved him, I know now! I just needed the security, I think. My parents died when I was 18, and I was on my own until I met him. It wasn't Doug I fell for – it was the idea of Doug, and everything he could offer me. A home, a family, our business, all binding me to another human being. Being part of something, not being alone any more. It wasn't fair to either of us. And now, after what happened, I wonder if he knew that too, deep down. I'm glad I found out before it was too late. It was an awful way to get a wake-up call, but maybe I needed one. It was the best thing for both of us. I need a fresh start. I need a new life. I need—"

"Leah," he said, sitting next to her and holding her wet hand in his. "Stop. I have to tell you, before you go on, that I'm not the man to give you what you need. Despite what just happened. Please don't ask it of me. I'm not capable. I'm broken. Parts of me don't work any more, and I don't think anyone can fix them. I like you, Leah. And, well, wow to the sex part. But more than that? I don't have it in me to give, and I don't want to lie to you. Not now, when you're hurting so bad; not ever. You deserve better than Doug. And you damn well deserve better than me."

Leah squeezed his hand, gazed up at him from tear-wet lashes.

Oh, she thought, he was so completely beautiful. As beautiful as a man could ever be. She lifted her hand, traced the hard outline of his jaw, and smiled. He might not be God, but he was definitely a gift from Him. A Christmas gift to give her hope, and friendship, and possibly multiple orgasms.

Tomorrow, or the next day, or the one after that, she knew she had to face her new reality. But right here, this was all she needed: the perfect distraction, and a salve for her pain. It wouldn't last, but then again, what did? Life, she had to accept, was a fragile beast: you could do your best to control it, but it was a wild thing, with a will of its own. There was no security, no certainty. People died. People betrayed you. So for now at least, she'd live in the moment.

"You don't know what I was going to say, Rob. And don't worry, one quick fumble in the kitchen doesn't mean I've fallen for you. But thank you, for your kindness, and your honesty. I don't expect anything of you, Rob. We don't even really know each other, and I certainly don't think you're my knight in shining armour. But we landed here, together, at this time, and well... call me an old hippy, but I think it was fate. That right here, right now, we can help each other. I don't need a boyfriend. Or a husband. Or a family – I need to learn to be me, without anybody else. Does that make sense?"

Rob nodded, gesturing for her to go on. He wanted to hear what she said – with Leah, he'd already learned to expect the unexpected.

"And as for parts of you not working," she said, " well, other parts of you definitely do work, so perhaps..." her hand trailed down to the lean muscle of his thigh, fingers stroking upwards, "we should concentrate on those. Let's have this one Christmas together. No expectations. No promises. We don't have a past, we don't have a future. We have the present. Just a lot of laughter, and some truly phenomenal sex. What do you say?"

"I say that sounds like the best Christmas I've had in years," he replied.

Chapter 5

"Now that," Leah said as she woke up, her tousled blonde head poking its way out from the duvet, "is a mighty fine view."

Rob was standing at the window, staring out into the fields. Completely naked. Those broad shoulders, bulked biceps; the smooth skin of his back rippling with lean muscle as he turned to smile at her. Tapered waist; the powerful length of his thighs. And right in the middle, the cherry on top of the pie, that utterly breath-taking backside. What a body. The kind she'd never seen anywhere but a movie screen before now.

She'd got to know every inch of it over the last three days. In great and glorious detail. The bag she had with her was intended for hand luggage, and contained a bumper pack of condoms tucked away for the honeymoon that never was. Another little Christmas miracle, and one that allowed them both to explore each other in ways that had left them tingling and exhausted. Three days of unparalleled pleasure, cocooned in their cottage in the snow.

"There's been a thaw," he said, turning to walk back over to the bed. Lord, he was magnificent. Every abdominal an awesome outline; every movement perfectly graceful; every flash of those dark brown eyes enough to make her wet. In a good way.

"You might," he said, climbing into bed next to her, "be able to leave soon. And I need to get back to work."

"Oh, well," said Leah, rolling next to him and reaching across to trace the hard contours of his muscled chest. Hard and muscled but covered in the most gorgeous velvety skin she'd ever touched. It hardly seemed fair it should belong to a man. "That's good news."

Was it? She wondered. She wasn't sure at all. She wasn't sure she wanted to leave this fantasy she was wrapped up in. She wasn't sure she wanted to leave this alternate reality they'd created together, where they were both safe from the stresses and pains of the outside world. It felt so right, being here with him. Exciting and peaceful all at the same time. Couldn't she just stay here forever, living an eternal Christmas with Rob Cavelli? Touching this amazing body, listening to that sexy American drawl, looking into those deep, pain-tinged eyes of his? No. She knew it couldn't last. They'd struck a deal, and going all clingy now wasn't part of it, no matter how much she wanted to. Even the thought of it ending brought her to the edge of tears, and that wasn't fair on him.

Instead, she ran her hand down over his chest, across the planes of his taut stomach to the ridge of his hip bone. That way, she knew, lay madness. Wonderful, soul-shaking, brain-busting madness.

"Go any lower and there'll be consequences," he said, his voice stern.

"That's what I was counting on," she replied, letting her hand drift casually down to stroke his already hard penis. It twitched in her hand and she smiled, trying and failing to circle its breadth with her fingers. Wow. The stuff of legend.

There was one condom left. It seemed a shame to waste it. Especially if this was going to be their last time. She shut that thought out of her brain. It didn't feel good, so she chose to ignore it.

She turned away from Rob, onto her side, presenting him with her back and pretending to yawn.

"You know what?" she said, smiling to herself, "I'm tired. It's going to be a long day. Let's get some sleep."

Silence. She stifled a laugh as she pictured his disbelieving face.

45

"Yeah? Too tired, huh?" he asked. She felt his long, lean body slide against hers; the press of his erection against her bottom; the warmth of his breath on her face as he pulled back her hair and nibbled her earlobe. His arm slipped under hers, his hand found her breast; rolling and teasing and stroking until her breath was coming in quiet bursts of anticipation.

He threw one leg across her hips, pinning her next to him, and she could feel the tip of his manhood sliding between her thighs. God, she knew a good place for that to go. She wriggled around, trying to catch the angle.

His mouth had moved to her neck; was working its magic across all those pleasure zones she never knew she had until he made them come alive. His hand stroked downwards, over her stomach, one finger trailing its way towards her centre. Ooh. Now that felt nice, she thought, stretching a little, feeling a now-familiar throb humming away inside her.

"If you're tired," he said, even the whisper of his words on her skin erotic, "you should take it easy."

He pulled away, and she started to protest. She'd never been any good at treating 'em mean.

"Shh," he said, rolling her over so she was lying face down, head resting on a plump goosedown pillow. "You just stay there, take a break – and let me do all the work."

She smiled into the pillow. Well. Who was going to argue with an offer like that?

She stretched her arms above her head, and he captured both her wrists in one of his hands, holding her still. His free hand roamed over her body; her neck; sliding round to her throat, over her shoulders. Skimming over her upturned bottom, down to her thighs. He followed the touch of his fingers with the touch of his lips, blazing fire all along Leah's body. She started to writhe, keen to participate now they'd started.

"No. Just stay still," he said, his voice low and husky. She was so beautiful, he thought, exploring every nuance, every hill; every dip and curve that made up the topography of her flesh. The falls and rises, and sweet, sweet valleys. So responsive, so generous, so god damn sexy. He'd never met a woman so naturally in tune with her body and its needs – she was totally uninhibited, greeting each experience, each orgasm, as though it was her first.

He placed his hand between her thighs. Slowly upwards, until he hit home. Used his fingers in the steady rhythm he knew drove her wild. Watched her yelp and twitch with pleasure as she came, clamping hard around him, eyes glazing and drifting away to wherever it was she went when she climaxed.

And now, he could tell from the wriggling of her peachy butt and the snuffling sounds she was making into the pillow, she was ready. More than ready. He slid the condom on, parted her legs, and plunged straight into her.

Leah pulled in breath. She hadn't expected that, she registered amid the shock and the pleasure. So quick, so sudden, so deep, when she was still tingling from the touch of his fingertips, still reeling from the pleasure-shock of her orgasm. And now he was inside her, so deep he might come out the other side. It felt glorious. Her hips rose and fell to meet his thrusts, her fingers clenching the pillow until her knuckles turned white. He was holding her hips now, raising her slightly as he kneeled behind her, plunging into her again and again, faster and faster, pounding at her pelvis with an animalistic need.

"More!" she said. "Give me more, Rob!"

Leah's words pushed Rob over the edge and he slammed into her furiously, over and over, growling her name as he exploded inside her. He fell forward, spent and sore and still shaking with one of the most mind-blowing orgasms he'd ever had. He rested his face against her sweat slicked back for a moment as he caught his breath, then turned her over, climbed on top, wrapped her body in his arms so tight he could have stood up and carried her. If his legs had been capable of movement, that is.

"Jesus, Leah," he said. "What was that?"

"I don't know," she murmured, voice muffled as she kissed his chest. "I was hoping you'd tell me. Certainly nothing that I've ever encountered before."

"Leah," he said, after they both regained their breath. "Come with me."

"*Again?* I'm not sure I'm capable yet. I'll need at least five minutes recovery time."

"No. Not that. Come with me. To Chicago."

Chapter 6

She'd assumed Rob said what he said because his brain was fried by great sex. It was afterglow talk, Leah thought; the kind nobody should ever be held accountable for. There should be some small print in legal documents stating you couldn't make life decisions in the fifteen minutes following orgasm.

But once it became clear that the weather was changing, and it was going to be possible to fly the next day, he stuck to his offer. Long after the hard-on had faded. That one, at least.

They were in the bathroom, and Leah was perched on the edge of the tub, watching in fascination as he went about the business of transforming himself into a totally different person.

"I don't mean as my lover," he said, meeting her eyes in the mirror. "You have to understand that."

Leah nodded, not really listening. They'd showered together, which had obviously taken a lot longer than it should. They were now both exceptionally clean and exceptionally satisfied. Leah had wrapped herself up in his big white cotton robe, and sat back to enjoy the show.

There was something terrifically intimate about watching a man go about his rituals. Especially shaving. Something masculine and erotic and arousing. Then again, she thought, she could probably watch this man do his shopping at Sainsbury's and find it erotic.

Especially in the fresh fruit aisle.

Inch by creamy inch, he was losing the thick, blue-black stubble that had coated his jawline since she'd known him.

He'd soon step out of the jeans and T-shirts and sweaters. Emerge as a clean-cut, hair-brushed, after-shaved, totally delectable creature in the impossibly chic charcoal grey suit he already had laid out on the bed.

He would look fantastic, but she wasn't all together sure she wanted the old Rob to say goodbye just yet. The new Rob already seemed more tense, and only half his facial hair was gone, washed down the drain along with all his easy charm. The new Rob was sharper, more business-like. Less happy.

This exceptionally white Christmas was ending, and like the snow outside the cottage, their blissful, fabricated world was melting away. Leah had no idea what would be left when the last drifts had gone.

He wanted her to come to Chicago, he'd said, and now he seemed to be laying down his ground rules. It was all a bit confusing, if she was honest; and not helped by the sight of his backside right at eye level in snug fitting white jersey boxers. What was a woman to do? She was supposed to be discussing life plans and all she could think about was sinking her teeth into those spectacularly sculpted cheeks.

It would probably help if she paid more attention to what he was actually saying and not what he – or his bottom — was doing. Listen up, Miss Harvey, she told herself – you may be tested afterwards.

"Okay, that's fine." she replied, on auto-pilot, looking up to his face. Now she was distracted by the way his golden skin contrasted with the brilliant white cotton of his shirt. Nightmare. She gave herself a mental slap.

"Sorry, Rob. I wasn't really listening. What did you say again? Once more for the dunce in the corner?"

He shook his head, looked a bit exasperated, and said: "I was explaining that if you decide to come, it won't be as my lover."

"Okay. What would I be then?"

"You'd be my... Hell, I don't know! But I do know you need a fresh start. A new life – you said it yourself. What better way to do that than in a different country? A different time zone? A different world?"

"But what will I do there? I've never been out of Europe. I was supposed to go to the Caribbean for my honeymoon, but, well, I got waylaid."

"You can cook, like you do here. I know you're talented, and I can tell you'd miss it if you gave it up. You're lucky to have a passion, and you should pursue it. I have a big business. I always need catering. I have meetings, parties, functions, dinners. Anything from two people to five hundred. You can start off with that, until you find your feet and get work of your own. I'll help you get started. But as a friend – no sex involved. We both move on."

"Move on." she echoed, quietly. Move on from this man. From his body. From his touch. From his warmth; his sense of humour, his kindness. His deeply buried pain that she'd never be able to heal. From her own past. The death of her parents. The marriage that never was. Move on from all of that – but also with him, to Chicago?

Was she capable of such a thing? She wasn't sure she was that good with change. There'd been too much change when she was younger, and clinging to Doug had been her way of avoiding it since.

Now she'd moved on to Rob Cavelli, the man who'd given her more orgasms in the last couple of days than anyone else in the rest of her life. The man who made her smile and laugh and feel good about herself.

The man who had been brutally honest about the fact he could never, ever love her. The no entry sign remained firmly in place – despite the enforced closeness of the last few days, their conversations had never left the realm of superficial and flirty.

51

He'd never mentioned his wife, and they'd avoided any topic likely to make one of them upset.

They'd been together – but not.

And now, he was offering her this amazing chance to recreate herself exactly at the time she needed it most, while at the same time telling her it was time to move on? What were his motives, she wondered? If he didn't want any more sex, was it out of friendship? Concern? Gratitude for a good lay? God only knew, and he wasn't telling.

She hadn't asked for any of this, but she needed to think about it. About herself, about her motivations – about the way she'd half lived her life up until now. She knew now, with the brutal surge of truth that hindsight brought, that she'd been piggy backing onto Doug's life for a long time. He offered her the security she needed, a ready-made existence she could move into that she'd thought of as safe. This man – this move to Chicago – would be far from safe, she knew. But the security of her previous life had all turned out to be a myth anyway.

She had to acknowledge to herself that she had, to some extent at least, used Doug. Not that it excused what he did on their wedding day, but, perhaps he'd sensed it without ever voicing it. She'd used him for security. For the chance to share her nights with someone who understood when the nightmares about her parents came.

He was older, he had a business, a home, a fully fledged existence for her to move straight in to. She'd never really tried to make it on her own. Becoming Doug's girlfriend had meant she never had to. She'd flailed around after her parents died, lost and lonely, and grasped at the chance to move in with him when they'd only been together for a few weeks. She'd never really learned to stand on her own two feet.

Maybe it was time to begin. Or at the very least to try. And Rob – Mr Not As A Lover – was offering her a head start.

She stood up decisively, grabbed the nearest towel, and tied it around his waist. She needed a clear mind. He raised his eyebrows at her in the mirror, but stayed quiet.

"Not as a lover. Okay, I get that. That would be important for both of us, the no bonking thing," she said, thinking it over. It was easier to concentrate now all that tanned, muscular flesh was covered up.

He was right. Of course he was right. She was never going to be independent if she was in Rob's bed every night, was she? She'd become a sex addict and have to go to support groups in church halls, for goodness' sake. And of course she could cook. Americans had to eat as well. It could be the best thing that ever happened to her, if she could pull it off. Her Christmas fantasy with Rob was over, but the rest of her life – with herself – could just be starting. It was an adventure. It was an opportunity. It was the freshest of fresh starts she could have imagined.

"Yes. You're definitely right. And if you can stick to it, so can I. I'll come with you, yes. I'll try and make it on my own, with a bit of help at the start. But before we do that moving on thing, Rob, before we give up the bedroom stuff, I have to say, for the record, that this has been the best bloody sex I've ever had. If you ever need, you know, a reference or anything, I'm your girl. Honestly, I've come so much in the last 24 hours I think I might have used up a year's supply."

"Ouch," he said, as his usually steady hand slipped with the razor. "Please don't talk like that while I have a sharp piece of metal held to my throat."

"Sorry! But while I have you as a captive audience, maybe I should make my big speech. This place has been magic, Rob. I know we can only ever be friends, and I'm okay with that. I don't need a relationship right now, with anyone other than me. I need to learn how to be independent again, how to enjoy my own company. How to be strong again, alone, for the first time since my parents died.

"But this has been special. No, don't talk, or nod – wouldn't want you to bleed out. You've said your piece, this is mine. The

53

last few days have been amazing. I've enjoyed all of it. Especially the naked parts. I've done things I've never even imagined. Things I didn't know were physically possible. Things that are probably illegal in some states of America.

"Now I know what's possible between a man and a woman, what sensational things my body is capable of feeling, well, I'll be looking for more of it. I mean, you can't be the only man in the world who makes me feel like that, can you? Maybe I've just been unlucky so far. I'll have to work my way through a few more 'til I hit gold again, probably kiss a few frogs before I find a prince, but I feel like for the first time, I understand why women obsess about sex as much as they do! So thank you. Not just for this offer, but for everything."

Rob was silent as she drew to the end of her ramble. Silent, he noticed, and covered in nicks from his shaving hand slipping again and again and again. Jesus, he thought, reaching for the towel. He was lucky he hadn't decapitated himself, listening to that speech. Sex. Orgasms. Nudity. And, other men? Kissing frogs? Kissing anyone?

He was fine with that he told himself, as he washed blood from his face. Absolutely fine. It was only natural she'd want to meet other men, and wasn't he the one who'd just been urging her to move on? And wasn't he apparently the one who'd unleashed her sense of lust? He'd stoked the fires, and now it was ready to rage through the unwitting male population of Chicago – how incredibly clever of him. Well, the male population would be very grateful. They'd probably erect a plaque, or build a statue in Grant Park.

But that was okay. He wouldn't have to watch. He doubted he'd be around in her life for long anyway – she'd spread her wings and fly within weeks. She had real talent; she had that great plummy accent going for her; that contagiously fun personality. Not to mention looking like a sex goddess you could pick up and carry round in your pocket. She'd find a new boyfriend without any problems, and... he was fine with it. Absolutely fine.

Chapter 7

The snow had cleared the very next day, enough for them to hike to the end of the path, where the magical two bars appeared on Rob's mobile. His driver arrived a few hours later, to whisk them both to the airport. If he wondered who the mystery girl was, he was too well-trained to ask. It was, Rob knew, ridiculously sudden – but somehow it also felt ridiculously right.

Leah just smiled at him nervously, feeling slightly slutty, and kept a tight grip of her handbag. Contents: make-up, phone (no charger), passport (thank God) and now, no condoms at all. The ultimate walk of shame.

Just days ago she should have been marrying Doug, and instead she was on her way to another country with a man she barely knew. Well, whatever happened when she got there, she knew one thing for sure – there was nothing left for her in London. Not Doug, definitely. Even if she didn't hate him quite as much as circumstances suggested she should, it was definitely over between them. She didn't have many close friends. Her parents were dead. There was no reason at all to stay – not when she'd had this weird and wonderful offer.

She'd realised, though, as soon as the car pulled up at the end of the path, that Mr Cavelli's world was very different from the world of 'her' Rob. Her Rob didn't shave for days on end, and slummed around in Levis and sweatshirts. Her Rob smiled and laughed and did very rude things to her. This Rob – the real Rob she supposed – was a different creature.

He was polite to the driver, but distant. He didn't even look twice at the fact that he was in a shiny black Porsche Cayenne. He didn't even notice when they did a drive-through check-in to the first-class departures lounge. He was too busy talking on his phone, using a language she didn't understand – Dow Jones and mergers and a type of footsie she was sure you couldn't play under the table.

There was a laptop, with a screen that seemed to cast some kind of magic spell – once the lid was lifted, Rob got sucked into an alternate universe. One that barely allowed him time to breathe, never mind eat, drink, converse or flirt.

Didn't stop him looking gorgeous, though, she noticed, flicking a glance at the man next to her, perfectly tailored shirt doing nothing to hide the bulk of his shoulders, long legs stretched a mile out in front of him. He sure wouldn't survive a nine-hour flight in economy.

Luckily, 'economy' didn't seem to be a word that applied in his world. The man she'd found hiding away in a remote stone cottage with its own dodgy generator was obviously rich. So much for living on cheese on toast and eking out a living as an artist. He may have issues – but money wasn't one of them.

At his insistence, at the airport she acquired a whole new suitcase of clothes. In a whole new suitcase. When she'd protested that she didn't have her cashcards with her and would make do with what she had, he just looked at her like she was insane.

"Right," he said. "That'll work. Which outfit are you planning to go for? The muddy wedding dress or the porn star T-shirt? Don't be crazy. I can afford it. There's a lot of money to be made in the reindeer business. And if you really want to, once you're settled, you can pay me back. Cook me dinner. Whatever."

It sounded sensible at the time, but as she surveyed the

shamefully thick bundle of receipts shoved into her bag, she wasn't so sure. They could prop up a wonky table leg, there were so many. The airport shops were in a strange post-Christmas, pre-New Year frenzy, decorations looking frayed around the edges and 'sale' signs starting to emerge. And by the time she'd finished, they were all severely depleted of stock. There were slinky new jeans; boots made of butter-soft leather; a cashmere coat that buttoned all the way up to her chin. Toiletries and underwear and a brand new phone. She felt like a footballer's wife, and was amazed at how much she enjoyed it. It seemed she was much more shallow than she'd ever realised. So much for independence.

Makeover aside, by the time they boarded, she was still feeling dazed to be sitting on a plane to Chicago. It felt surreal. Like it was happening to somebody else.

It had been a rollercoaster of a week. Her whole life had been turned upside down, and to her surprise, she was enjoying the topsy turvy view a lot more than the old one. She was starting to wonder if she had some kind of personality disorder. It was like a switch had been flicked inside her; all the pain and turmoil had been blocked out, replaced by a sense of hope and excitement and pleasant confusion. She'd gone from ruined bride to bright-eyed émigré in just a few days. Entirely possibly, she knew, she was heading for a giant fall. She'd been running full-pelt on adrenaline and sex this week, and that was the kind of fuel that never got you very far.

There was still so much she needed to do, she thought, as she settled down for the journey. Talk to Doug mainly; and be a grown-up about it. Face up to the conversation she was dreading having. Get her stuff shipped over. Talk to her bank. Boring, necessary things; things she didn't want to even think about right now.

This was the start of a whole new phase in her life. A phase where she could recreate herself. Be the strong, independent woman she wanted to be. Get her own flat. Her own job. Learn about a new culinary tradition – Chicago urban. Gourmet deep pan and posh hot dogs and the blend of cultures and tastes that all brewed up in US cooking.

She'd make new friends. Explore new places. Take up yoga. Grow her own herbs. Learn to play the violin. And, she added to the list, buy a bloody big vibrator – because the fragrant man-God next to her had opened floodgates she never wanted to close.

He looked so stern, so serious; his dark head bent to the laptop, his fingers tapping a tense rhythm on the arm rest. If ever a body was created to carry a suit, it was his. Everything fitted so perfectly. Shirt open a couple of buttons at the top, silky black hair just peeking out. Midnight shadow already starting to spread across the hard line of his jaw. Lush.

The only problem with flying first class, Leah decided, was the leg room. There was just too damn much of it. No excuses to bump hips; touch thighs, or accidentally fall asleep on the firm ridge of a shoulder.

"You're staring at me," he said, not moving his eyes from the screen. "Are you thinking bad things?"

"Of course not," she replied. "We're just friends these days, Rob. No hanky panky allowed. I look at you and I see nothing. I feel nothing. And I certainly do not, under any circumstances, imagine asking for a blanket, throwing it over your lap, putting my hand down your pants and giving you some in-flight entertainment."

He sighed, loudly. Paused. Slammed the lid of the computer shut.

"Jesus, Leah," he said. "What are you trying to do to me?"

Her gaze flickered down to his groin. Sure enough, the material of his trousers was starting to tent in a very satisfying way. She felt an answering throb beating somewhere in her La Senza knickers, and realised no sex toy was ever going to come up to these standards.

"Hmmm. That's a good question. Do you fancy visiting the loo with me? Then we can figure out exactly what it is I'm trying to do to you? The way I see it, we're not in Chicago yet. The just friends thing shouldn't really start until then... I mean, we're still in international air space. There's probably some kind of diplomatic treaty that says it's okay for us to have one last tumble."

He met her look. As usual, he felt any resolve he thought he had soften in direct correlation to other parts of him becoming hard. Maybe she was right. One more for the road? Not classy, that's true; but something about the idea of a quickie in close quarters had a certain appeal. He smiled, and his hand reached out to hers. What the hell...

She climbed over him, clambering into the aisle and casting him a saucy look as she went. How long should he give it, he wondered, before he followed?

He was halfway out of his seat when the familiar ding of the announcement bell sounded.

"Ladies and gentlemen," came the slow, rehearsed drone of the pilot's voice, "we've made excellent time on our flight today, and I'm pleased to tell you we'll be touching down in Chicago forty minutes ahead of schedule. Please return to your seats and put on your seatbelts in preparation for our descent and landing. Cabin crew will be round shortly."

Oh, thought Leah, locked away in the first class bathroom, top already halfway over her head. Bummer.

Chapter 8

"It looks like Oz. I should be wearing ruby red shoes..." she murmured, gazing out of the window of the limousine.

They'd been picked up by Rob's chauffeur at O'Hare International, and for the first twenty minutes or so, the drive had been disappointingly bland. For an exciting start to a new life, it had all looked amazingly dull – flat landscape, the usual advertising hoardings, little in the way of greenery. She could have been in any suburb, anywhere. It looked like Heathrow, with more snow.

Then, as they neared the centre of Chicago proper, it appeared in front of them, all at once: a shimmering city of skyscrapers, man-made towers of steel and brick reaching up to touch the dusky-grey December heavens; concrete fingers stretching high to poke the sodden clouds.

It was breath-taking.

The car navigated its way through a mass of streets; jumbled, older neighbourhoods on the outskirts, into the massive, authoritarian thoroughfares of the Loop business district. More towers; a row of moving steel bridges over the Chicago River; offices and stores and coffee shops and apartment buildings and tiny pocket parks tucked away in hidden corners. Snow on the pavements, ice on the trees, frost on the cars. And the people. Scurrying around in the last of the light, dashing from one place to another, like busy worker ants sheltering under their umbrellas, collars turned up against the cold. Christmas lights draped from trees, coated in snow, glowing festive through the murky grey glimmer of late afternoon.

"What do you think?" Rob asked. He'd been telling her about the city as they drove; about its history, about its architecture; its food and music and art. His passion was endearing – how could she do anything but love it?

"It's amazing," she replied. "Brilliant. What's that?" she said, pointing to an enormous building off to their left. It was so high she couldn't even see the top of it through the limo's windows.

"It's the Willis Tower," he said. "Used to be called the Sears Tower. Tallest building in the States. Cavelli Tower is near here, on Dearborn Street. Not quite as big as the Willis, but size doesn't matter. Or so I'm told."

"Actually," she replied, still staring out at the vibrant city streets. "Size does matter. That's a lie women tell to make men feel better."

"Darn. I always suspected. Any complaints?"

She turned back to him. Smiled in a way that made his heart lurch and his crotch stir.

"Well, we're in Chicago now, and officially just friends, so I don't want to flirt too much. But if you were a Chicago building? The Willis Tower would be feeling emasculated."

The car drew to a halt before he could respond, which was probably a good thing, Rob decided. Because if he was a Chicago building, he was growing a couple of extra levels with every passing second.

The driver got out, opened the door, and passed Rob an open umbrella.

He held it over Leah's head as they walked towards the glass doors to the lobby of his office building; another skyscraper, one which doubled as office and home for both Rob and his brother Marco.

The car pulled silently off, taking their cases around to the service lift. Leah assumed they'd be whisked away, up to Rob's apartment in the penthouse. Don't get too used to this lifestyle, young woman, she reminded herself – you'll be living in a rat-infested fleahole and surviving on microwave rice once you get this whole independent woman thing sorted.

"Welcome to my humble abode," said Rob, guiding her towards the entrance, his hand in the small of her back as they walked towards the lobby.

The doors slid open, and Leah saw elegant fittings; dark wood; framed paintings. Old charm combined with cutting edge technology. Freestanding vases filled with stunning floral arrangements. A genuine fire blazing in the corner. A bank of security cameras; a computerised info point with a touch screen, three separate sets of doors to the lifts. A polished mahogany concierge desk. Coffee tables piled high with glossy magazines surrounded by stylish, comfortable sofas.

And, in the middle of all of this, four burly men. In uniform. With guns. And batons. And tasers.

"Mr Roberto Cavelli?" one of them said, stepping forward, his voice flat and calm and ever so slightly menacing.

"Yes?" Rob replied, clearly concerned. Leah tightened her grip on her bag; flooded with the sense of foreboding that the emergency services always provoked in her. Ever since the day when she was eighteen, and that knock on the door came. The one that told her about the fire that had killed her parents. The policewoman they'd sent was young and kind, but that hadn't changed the brutality of the news.

Was this bad news? For Rob? For someone he loved?

"Mr Cavelli," the cop said, walking forward, unhooking a set of plastic handcuffs from his waistband. "You need to come with us. You're under arrest. You have the right to remain silent..."

Chapter 9

"So. Am I in trouble?" asked Rob, trying to manoeuvre his bound wrists into a more comfortable position. One that maybe involved blood flowing into his hands.

He was sitting on a hard plastic chair, in a hard plastic room, somewhere inside a hard brick police station. Outside, he could see Leah having an animated conversation with the officer who'd arrested him; arms flying, hands waving, eyes huge, body fizzing with energy. You go girl, he thought. You'll talk him to death if nothing else.

"Yeah," replied his brother Marco, perched on the table next to him, sipping coffee so bad it made him wince. "And I'll tell you why. You've been arrested. You're sitting in an interview room in cuffs. You're facing charges of kidnap and assault. And all you've done since I got here is watch that woman's ass through the door. So yeah, bro, I'd say you were in pretty big trouble, one way or another. What the hell's going on?"

Rob grinned up at Marco, who was looking spectacularly un-attorney like in his sweats and dirt-stained T-shirt. He'd called his cell as soon as the cops let him use his phone, and rudely interrupted his traditional festive period activity of playing football in the park with their cousins. Usually fun, usually violent, and always, always muddy. It was a boy thing.

"Wish I could tell you, Marco. But I'm not even sure myself. She just walked into my life. Christmas Eve. Turned up like a magic fairy on the doorstep. I've told you, I couldn't turn her away. She'd have died."

"I get that," said Marco. "I do. I even get that she stayed a couple days because of the weather. Where I start to get confused is the part where you assault her, and coerce her into coming to Chicago with you."

"Oh for Christ's sake, Marco, you know me better than that! There was no coercion involved – in any of it! It was all consensual. Just two consenting adults who..."

Rob trailed off, not wanting to kiss and tell, even in his current circumstances.

"What? What did you consent to?" probed Marco. "Roberto Paolo Cavelli, have you been, and I'll phrase this diplomatically, *intimate* with that woman? *You?* At Christmas?"

Rob's expression told Marco everything he needed to know. Guilty as charged, your honour, he decided. Marco didn't know whether to call the psych ward or go outside and shake Leah Harvey's hand. His brother had shunned pretty much all human contact at Christmas for the last three years, never mind shared a bed with someone. There'd been women, obviously, but never at Christmas. That was sacred, untouchable. He glanced outside, saw the small blonde woman still going off at the cops like a pocket rocket. Okay, she was pretty. Hot, in fact. But Rob got a lot of offers from hot women – what made this one so special that he broke the yuletide embargo for her? Blackmail? Witchcraft? Rohypnol?

As he pondered, the door to the interview room flew open, pushed so hard it thudded back into the wall with a crash. Patches of bare plaster chip around the hinges said it wasn't the first time that had happened, and it probably wouldn't be the last.

Leah strode in, eyes flashing with fury, hands on hips, chest heaving with restrained anger. The harassed look on the police-man's face made it clear she'd come pretty close to getting arrested herself. She'd probably only avoided it because Officer Karlsson was enjoying the heaving chest as much as the next man.

"This is my brother, Marco," Rob said, nodding towards his twin.

Leah paused, giving Marco a quick glance and a polite 'pleased to meet you' and acknowledging how similar they looked before returning her eyes to Rob. She could barely see anything else, she was so angry. She stared at the bloody handcuffs, chafing into his flesh. Okay, maybe one day, handcuffs would be fun, she thought – but this was neither the time nor the place, and she was so angry she thought her brain might come out of her ears. He really didn't deserve this.

"It's because of the car," she said. "After I walked out on the wedding, Doug couldn't get me on the phone. He drove for hours looking for me, then eventually went back to London, expecting to find me there. When there was no sign of me, he freaked out.

"It's kind of my own fault – I should have found a way to let him know I was okay. But I didn't, and he had a big dollop of guilty conscience to add into the mix as well. So he called the police and reported me missing! They traced the car, and came to check at your cottage in case you'd seen me. By this point I think they expected me to be dead under a snow drift or something. Instead, they found, er," she flushed slightly, avoiding Marco's piercing gaze, "they found signs of activity. In the bedroom. The ruined wedding dress. And my blood, in the kitchen. From—"

"The god-damn broken plate!" Rob said, everything falling into place and making slightly more sense. "But they can see you're okay now, can't they? What's the problem?" he added.

"The problem is Doug. He's convinced I've been abducted or something ridiculous and, well, I suppose he's been really worried. For days. Thinking maybe I'd topped myself or something because of what he did. So I've been explaining to Officer Karlsson here that I am duress-free, here because I very much want to be, and that a couple of hours ago I was trying to persuade you to have sex with me in a bloody aeroplane toilet!"

The last word was delivered three notes higher than the rest, and Leah's wide eyes filled with tears of frustration. What a great start to her new life – getting the man who was making it all possible arrested, because she'd been too stubborn and too dumb to bother letting Doug know she was alive and well and having her brains bonked out by a gorgeous American stud. Or at least the first two parts.

It was understandable that she hadn't wanted to talk to Doug. Especially given all the bonking, and the genuine lack of phone signal. But she could still have called from the airport. Even just texted him. Now, as well as having got Rob into this trouble, she even felt a twinge of guilt at how worried Doug must have been.

"I'm so sorry, Rob," she said, holding his cuffed hands up to her mouth and kissing the sore skin of his wrist. "I'm nothing but bad news."

Marco watched as Rob stared into those tear-filled amber eyes, reassuring her it was all okay. He hadn't seen that look on his brother's face for...well, for ever.

"Leave this to me, guys," he said, sliding off the graffiti-scarred table and leaving the room.

***

Less than an hour later, the three of them were sitting at a secluded corner table at a restaurant called Giordano's on Jackson Boulevard. In front of them was possibly the largest pizza Leah had ever seen. It was, she'd been informed, stuffed, not deep pan – the subject of much distinction in the Chicago food world. And it was also, she'd been told, known as a 'pie'.

A pie the size of a small planet, she thought, staring it down. It was the enemy, and would be defeated.

"Thanks, Marco, for getting us out of there. For some reason you were able to manage it when I couldn't," she said, scooping a slice of pie onto her plate. Steaming hot cheese oozed out, and the delicious smell of mushrooms and garlic wafted towards her. Yum.

"Yeah," he answered. "For some reason, those cop guys listened more to a kick-ass Chicago-born attorney than a crazy English chick. Go figure."

"Ha. The swines; sexist *and* racist," she replied cheerfully, taking a mouthful and looking across at the two brothers facing her. Rob hadn't mentioned his twin, and now she was calm enough to see straight, she realised there were distinct advantages.

They had the same wide, sculpted lips. The same strong jaw; cheekbones you could cut yourself on. But there were some differences as well. Marco was bigger – not taller, but more brawn, more bulk, more brazenly built. Rob's body was that of an athlete, all sleek, lean muscle; Marco's of a football player. In-your-face beefcake. His hair was cut shorter, brutally cropped to his scalp, which meant either he was fresh out of the Marines (which she knew he wasn't), or it grew big and curly if he let it. The eyes. Again, not the same. Rob's were chocolate and gold; Marco's hazel. Not identical. But still twins. And still both drop-dead gorgeous.

Double yum.

She realised they'd both stopped talking as she carried out her totty inspection. Mildly embarrassing. She didn't even have score cards to hold up.

"So, what do you think? Do we pass muster?" asked Marco, breaking the silence.

"Oh God, don't ask her that. She'll only tell you." groaned Rob, burying his face in his hands. Leah gave him a look and laid down her knife and fork next to her plate.

"Well," she said, "if you insist, I was actually thinking that you two bring a whole new meaning to the phrase Italian beef sandwich. And that being the filling wouldn't be a totally awful experience at all."

Marco stared at her in disbelief, pizza slice paused midway to his mouth. Rob snorted, the sound muffled by his hands. "Told you so," he muttered. "There's no filter, Marco. She thinks it, she says it."

"Okay, fair enough," said Marco, recovering his composure. "I can respect that. While we're being honest, then, Leah – why are you here?"

There was an edge to his voice she couldn't help but notice. Not aggression, not exactly, but a note of warning. She understood. He was protective of Rob. He didn't know her, or her motives, and wanted to let her know he was watching out for him. Leah didn't have siblings herself, but if she did, she hoped they'd react like that. She felt a twinge of loneliness tug at her. Parents dead; Doug over, friends minimal. There was no-one in the world to look out for her like that. Rob was lucky, and she hoped he knew it.

"Marco, don't—" started Rob, obviously knowing his twin well enough to sense the hidden meaning behind his words. His eyes flew to Marco's, sparking with his own warnings, clenched fists slamming down onto the table top.

"No, it's fine Rob; in fact it's a good question," she said gently, holding out a hand to his to calm him. The last thing she wanted to do was cause a rift between brothers. Particularly when she had no place in their lives at all, other than a passing moment. She'd be gone before they could say double pepperoni, and that was probably a good thing for all of them.

"Marco, in all honesty I don't know why I'm here. Like you said, I'm just a crazy English chick. My life got turned upside down, and I discovered I liked it better that way. I won't bore you with the details, but not many people get the chance to turn things round like this, and that's what your brother's given me the opportunity to do. Yes, okay, so I've spent the last few days as his slave. Cooking for him, cleaning for him —"

"Give me a break!" said Rob, the corners of his eyes starting to crinkle in laughter.

"Cooking for him, cleaning for him, providing him with first-rate sex..." she continued, as though he'd never spoken, "and in return, Marco, he's been kind to me. He's offered me a chance to escape when I most need it. He's offered me a place to stay and a job until I find my feet. He's offered me friendship. He's also made it more than clear that's what we have – friendship. He doesn't want more than that. I don't want more than that. We're not a couple. I'm not looking for a boyfriend. Or a husband. I'm not looking to hurt him in any way. I'm just grateful that I met him. So. What do you think? Do I pass muster?"

There was silence again. The background noise of clinking glassware; steam from coffee machines; laughter and chatter and chairs scraping against wooden flooring.

"Yeah," said Marco, smiling. "You pass muster with me, Leah. But tomorrow, there'll be a bigger test."

"What's that?"

"Mom called earlier," said Marco, looking back to his brother. "She heard you got your ass hauled off to the copshop and she'll be round for breakfast."

"Oh shit."

Chapter 10

Dorothea Cavelli was not what Leah expected. Admittedly, all her preconceptions of a widowed Italian American matriarch were based on watching *The Godfather* movies – and Dorothea was about as far removed from that as it was possible to be.

She was in her late 60s, but looked nowhere near it. Her hair was pure snowy white, and cut thick into a funky, chunky bob. Her eyes were a glacial green, and her make-up was applied with understated precision. She wore a knee-length purple sweater dress over designer jeans, coupled with bohemian costume jewellery.

She was also, Leah realised with mounting concern, quite, quite serious.

"It's just a small affair," she said, sipping her coffee and crossing elegantly long legs. "Family, friends, some business colleagues. We'll have it here, in fact. It's big enough."

"Will we? Is it?" asked Rob, pouring himself a cup too. He looked exhausted, Leah thought, watching the way he sank down into the chair, rubbing his eyes as though he was still half asleep. Smart suit, white shirt, navy tie; perfectly co-ordinated with jet lag, adrenaline and fatigue. She'd spoken to Doug, sorted out the misunderstanding without getting too deeply into it and promised to call him back. But it had still been a tough day, and it had clearly taken its toll on Rob.

She didn't feel much better herself, but at least she didn't have to go to work on top of it all. At least, she hadn't thought she did, until Mrs Cavelli revealed her plans for a New Year party. A party that urgently needed a caterer. She'd moved impressively fast: she could only possibly have found out what Leah did for a living the night before, and was already in action. Leah could almost feel the silky touch of a web being weaved around her.

Ideally she needed nothing but sleep today. About ten hours, preferably drug induced and dream free. That'd perk her up no end. Maybe then, she'd feel up to a few rounds with Mama Cavelli, who was still talking. Maybe then, she might be able to unravel the tangle of emotions she was feeling after her first night as 'just friends' with Rob – which hadn't ended up all that friendly.

They'd got back at stupid o'clock, after a night of contrasts: cop shop, restaurant, impromptu tour of Chicago waterfront. The adrenaline of the day, and the fact her body clock thought it was still the afternoon, had kept her going through it all.

When they arrived back at Cavelli Tower, Rob showed Leah to her new apartment. The one she'd stay in until Marco sorted her temporary work visa.

There were two large suites on the penthouse floor, which belonged to Rob and Marco. Marco also had his own home, 'out by the Lake', wherever that was, only using the penthouse when he was working in town, or romancing the ladies – which was about eight nights a week, from what Rob had said. No surprises there – young, fit, single and gorgeous. There was probably a waiting list of nubile wenches with crampons and ropes trying to scale the walls of the Tower. For both of the Cavelli men, she thought, feeling a tight clench in her gut.

On the floor below the penthouses were two plush guest apartments, kept ready for visiting VIPs – corporate partners, potential customers, politicians, overseas guests, investors. Random waifs and strays rescued from blizzards.

"Wow," she'd said, grateful to be somewhere she could call

home, at least temporarily. "This is plush. This must be for real reindeer bigwigs. Haven't you got a broom cupboard somewhere in the cellar I could use instead?"

The place was stunning. Floor to ceiling windows with views across the tower-scape of the city. A sumptuous marble bathroom suite so decadent Marie Antoinette could have moved in. A TV bigger than a cinema screen. And a bed the size of a football pitch. A bed that would be totally wasted on her.

Rob had taken her in after Marco had gone off to his own rooms, shown her around, given her the keys. He'd stood in the doorway for a while first, his face dark and brooding, frowning as he watched her potter around, pressing buttons, opening cupboards and 'ooh-ing' and 'aah-ing' like a kid at the circus. Like she'd never seen anything as thrilling as a toothbrush glass before in her whole life.

She knew it was crazy, and she was definitely coming off as someone who might need Men in White Coats on her speed dial, but she couldn't help it. Once they were alone, she wasn't sure how to react, how to behave. She was nervous, on auto-twitter. Still cringing inside at the fact that she had, however unintentionally, got him arrested.

It had been a long and stressful day. A day that had wound its way slowly and inexorably to that point; almost midnight, near the top of a tower in the Windy City. The two of them there, together – with a bloody big bed winking at them, its silky sheets practically begging to be tumbled on. In days gone by, they'd have tumbled it to within an inch of its life, but things were different now.

No matter how much that bed was winking, she had to ignore it. A deal was a deal. Sticking to the deal, though, was costing a lot more than she expected. All she really wanted to do was to fall onto that bed with him, and sleep safe in his arms. Arms that were now off limits.

"Leah, you need to know that now I'm back here, I'll be busy," he said, still watching her from the doorway. "I've been away from work for almost two weeks, and there'll be a lot of catching up to do."

She nodded, appearing to be far more captivated by the remote control that opened and closed the drapes than anything he had to say.

"I'll be heading to the office tomorrow, and I work long hours. Don't expect to see much of me. If you need any help, I'll make sure the concierge staff are on hand."

"Great," she said, barely looking up, concentrating instead on the whooshing sound the drapes made as they opened and closed. "Thanks. And I can always ask Marco if I see him around."

A terse nod from Rob, a snap of suit fabric as he crossed his arms sharply in front of him. A distinctly peed off crease between his eyes, leaving her wondering what she had done wrong. It had been easy, when Marco was around, to keep her distance. To maintain her balance. Now, though, with just the two of them – well, she thought she might wobble over at any moment.

"I'm sure Marco will be only too pleased to help," he snapped. "Goodnight then – I'll leave you to stroke the soft furnishings."

Oh God, she thought. I've offended him somehow. When really I just want to hide the fact that I'm feeling embarrassed and vulnerable and altogether out of my depth.

What is the right etiquette for this situation, she wondered? For living under the same roof as the man she'd been sleeping with for the last few days? The man who was insistent he'd had enough of that arrangement, and who'd now declared himself a sex-free zone?

The logical part of her knew he was right. To continue would be madness. And, she thought, looking around at her luxurious surroundings, she'd start to feel a bit like a prostitute, or at least a modern-day courtesan, kept in a gilt-edged cage in return for servicing her master. A bit like Julia Roberts in Pretty Woman, but about two foot shorter.

The sex in Scotland had been fantastic: the perfect time, the perfect place; both healing and distracting; a moment taken out of reality for both of them. Now, though, they were here, back in this very real world of his, and she needed to find the 'off' switch. He didn't want her, he'd made that clear enough, and she, well, she only wanted him a little bit. Nothing she couldn't control, if she worked really really hard at it. And concentrated on the remote control instead.

That was the theory, at least. And it was a good theory. The reality, though, was him, filling up that doorway. Dark eyes and silky hair and long, lean legs leading up to the world's most perfect bum. Brooding away like an enigma wrapped up in a mystery wrapped up in the world's biggest hunk. The reality was knowing he could scoop her up in his arms like she was nothing, hold her to the stone velvet of his chest, throw her on that stupidly large bed and treat her like a courtesan. That she'd cry and scream and moan and respond to every touch he chose to give her. And that afterwards, she could lie in his arms, feeling as warm and safe as a child.

How did she make the mental switch from that to just friends? Where was the self-help guide for that? Should she give him a peck on the cheek? Invite him for a coffee, in his own building? Lock herself in the walk-in wardrobe and say the Lord's Prayer?

In the end Rob saved her the stress of deciding. He gave her a look that spoke of his own frustration, and slammed the door behind him on his way out.

Well, she'd thought, turning back to unpack her suitcase, that went well.

***

She had a restless night, tortured by dreams about Rob and Doug, and a scary interchanging of faces and body parts. Dreams about sex and food and jumping from a jet with a parachute that turned into a boa constrictor. And, inevitably she supposed, about her parents. They were never far from her thoughts, but times of stress

74

always made the nightmares worse. Leah had woken soaked with sweat and tears, heart pounding in her chest, the image of them trapped in their smoke-filled hotel room seared into her mind. Again. But this time, alone – no Doug to stroke away the tears and whisper comforting words. Nobody at all.

The dreams were always the same, always so vivid. It seemed like she could taste the acrid smoke clogging her throat; feel their panic as they realised what was happening; touch the jammed lock that led to the fire escape they never reached. She couldn't, of course. She had never even seen the hotel room. She'd been at home enjoying herself when her parents died, assuming the worst thing that would happen to her the next day was a killer hangover. And still, in her dreams, she saw it all through their eyes. Felt it all through their lungs.

Leah knew the drill by now. No point trying to sleep again after that. Get up, get active, get distracted. Until the next time. There would always be a next time.

As a result, she'd been up since five and was running on three hours of bad sleep and a reservoir of better coffee. She'd sat up in bed, watching local TV news anchors talk about the weather and the plans for New Year fireworks over the river. It was fascinating, even watching rubbish telly in a different culture – the accents, the language, the huge hair, the dazzlingly white teeth. Perfect zombie fodder.

The phone had started to ring at about 7am. She stared at it for a few moments, wondering if it was Rob. Wondering how she felt about that. Wondering if he was still angry, for reasons as yet unspecified.

When she finally dragged herself far enough across the bed to answer it, the voice on the other end introduced itself as Artie, the family's private concierge. Artie seemed like a really nice chap, but there was still a plume of disappointment curling its way down her stomach. Of course it wouldn't be Rob. He was far too busy and important now. She was just an item on his to-do list, a package to be taken care of. Passed on to the staff.

Her presence was required, Artie explained, in the drawing room. She had an audience with Mrs Cavelli. Those were his exact words: 'an audience with Mrs Cavelli'. As she climbed out of bed and padded barefoot to the wardrobe, Leah wondered if would be like the cabaret shows at home, and whether she'd be allowed to ask showbiz questions at the end.

She threw on some of her new jeans, and a stripy Marc Jacobs sweater she'd fallen in love with at the airport. Bit tight across the chest, but hey, what wasn't? Brush through the hair, touch of make up to hide dark circles under the eyes. A spritz of Jo Malone. Holy water and cross. Ready to go, prepared for anything Mrs Cavelli could throw at her. Not.

She'd found her way to the drawing room, which came with yet more stunning river views, and a vast balcony wrapped around the outside of the building. Rob was there – she hadn't been sure about that – and she nodded at him with a lot more vigour than she felt, choosing a seat as far away from him as she could to avoid the temptation to sit on his lap. Within minutes, Dorothea had dumped the small talk, and started filling her in on her plans for New Year-based social domination.

It seemed, quite scarily, that Leah was being professionally engaged by his equally scary mother to cater a party she'd suddenly decided to pull together. Words like shrimp and satay and smoked salmon were being bandied about, so she assumed that's what was happening. That, or Dorothea Cavelli was suffering from food-based Tourette's.

"Mother, how many people exactly are you thinking of, for this imaginary party?" said Rob, running his hands through his hair in frustration as he spoke. He knew he'd left furrows. He needed a haircut. He always did when he got back from Scotland, where he let himself turn into Grizzly Adams for a fortnight, but it usually wasn't an issue. He usually didn't have a woman he was sexually infatuated with in tow. And he usually didn't get arrested

by Chicago's finest the minute he walked through the door either. 'Usually' seemed to be a thing of the past with Leah on the scene.

It had been a tough night, and he was feeling the strain. He was tired; he'd been arrested, and now he had to go to work – but not without an audience with his mother first. Plus it was Christmas, and he always felt like crap at Christmas. His time with Leah had gone some way to distracting him from that, but now it was over, and he was paying for it with the guilt hangover from hell.

It hadn't helped that Leah had disappeared off into a world of her own once he took her to the guest apartment last night. It was like watching someone with functioning catatonia – she was walking and talking, but in a parallel universe; a universe that didn't involve him at all. It involved exclamations of delight about everything from the sofa fabric to the potpourri, and absolutely zero eye contact with him. Which was, of course, fine. He'd already learned that eye contact with Leah could end up with them naked in five minutes flat. He couldn't allow their affaire to continue – for both their sakes. Nothing could ever come of it; nothing good anyway. Even the fact that he wanted her so much, on a purely physical level, felt like a betrayal of Meredith and all they'd shared.

Since her death, there'd been other women. Lots of other women. But never for more than a night, and none of whom had inspired the kind of hunger he felt when he looked at Leah. The almost physical pain he felt when she left the room. That moment of complete paralysis when she'd said that silly thing about him and Marco in Giordano's; even knowing it was just her usual honest flirtiness, that she meant nothing by it. There'd been one split second where it entered his dumb brain that she might fin Marco just as attractive as she found him. The question he could quite find an answer for was why he cared. If he didn't want why shouldn't she go for Marco instead? He quelled a chur in his gut, like someone had slipped ground glass into his c

It was only physical. He had to remind himself of that. A lust. Nobody would ever replace Meredith, and losing cont

77

Leah would be futile and potentially damaging to them both. He was broken. He could not be fixed. He didn't want to be fixed; he didn't deserve it.

"Only about 60 or so, darling," his mother replied, jolting him back to reality.

"I see. Just a few dozen of your closest friends, right? Don't they have plans already? I don't know if it's occurred to you, mother, but there tend to be a lot of parties on New Year's Eve."

"Don't be ridiculous, Roberto – if they have other plans, they'll cancel, darling, and come here instead. I can't help thinking that Leah landing here just when I was toying with the idea of a soiree must be fate; a trained chef living under the Cavelli roof just when I need it! Do you think you're up to it, honey?"

His mother's gaze swivelled back to Leah, who was looking increasingly like Jessica Rabbit caught in the headlights of a large, unstoppable truck. A truck wearing Chanel No 5 and stiletto-heeled boots. He'd been there many times himself, and empathised with the look of frozen horror on her face.

Knowing his mother – the truck – as well as he did, and knowing Leah – a rabbit with bite – as well as he did, he suspected this could be entertaining. Shame Marco was missing out on this one. He smiled into his coffee, sat back, and waited for the fireworks.

"Yes. That does seem like an amazing coincidence," replied Leah, her tone making it perfectly clear that she recognised the smell of horse manure when she heard it. "Do *you* think I'm up to it, Mrs Cavelli? You're the client."

"Well I barely know you, sweetheart, but Rob seems to think so. And he's generally a very good judge of character. I taught him everything I know. So come on, quit stalling – are you up for it or not?"

Leah thought she might explode into smithereens. It was like being pinned back against the chair by a laser beam. She just couldn't get the size of Dorothea Cavelli at all – friend, foe or just plain freaky? So far she was playing it safe and sticking with

that last one.

But freaky or not, it sounded like her kind of challenge – crazy, spontaneous, and potentially a total train wreck. Exactly like the rest of her life. She had nothing to lose and everything to gain – and doing a good job for the family might go some way to making her feel less beholden to Rob for everything he'd done for her so far.

"Okay," she said. "Why not? I'm game if you are. And I don't exactly have a lot else to do this week."

As soon as she'd agreed, Leah screwed her nose up, looking off to the side in concentration, biting on her lower lip as she thought it through. "We need to decide menus. I'll need some advice on where to buy the produce. I'll need staff to help. I'll need—"

"Marvellous!" said Dorothea, clapping her hands together like an Indian raj dismissing her wallah. "We'll get to the details later. I'm glad you said yes, Leah. I'm sure you'll do a great job."

Yeah, Leah thought, unfurling her legs and stretching out, but if I don't – death by firing squad. And if all the other firing squads already have plans, they'll cancel, darling, and come here instead.

"Now, that's business out of the way. So, tell me all about yourself, Leah." said Mrs Cavelli, leaning forward eagerly.

"I hate to interrupt," said Rob, in a tone that implied exactly the opposite. He lifted his gaze from the newspaper he'd been pretending to read, and looked out at Leah. "But you don't need to do this, Leah. I didn't bring you here to be our slave, and I know you must be exhausted. You don't need to cater her party, and you don't need to tell her anything about yourself. My mother is just an old bully – don't let the act scare you."

There was a pause. An unearthly quiet as Dorothea Cavelli's face fell into the smooth, untroubled expression she usually wore right before she gave out an almighty ass-whooping. Ooops, thought Rob, I'm in for it now. Never too grown-up for an ass-whooping.

"Less of the old, sonny," she snapped. "And Leah – I haven't bullied you have I? You're not scared of me, are you?"

"Well, no," said Leah, standing up to leave. "I'm a grown woman after all. I don't scare that easily. But for a minute there, I was rather fearful for the fur of my hundred and one pet Dalmatians. See you later, guys. Mrs Cavelli – let me know when you have time to discuss the details."

She waltzed from the room without a further word. Rob swore she gave an extra swing to her hips as she went, and just knew, without a shadow of a doubt, that she'd be grinning her face off and stifling a laugh.

He looked back to his mother. Cruella, as he would call her from now on. Stately, elegant, beautiful. Legs crossed. Hands crossed. Eyes almost crossed. With laughter.

"My God Rob," she said, when the tide subsided and she was able to breathe again. "Where the hell did you find her? And is there a spare one for Marco?"

No, he thought, clamping down on an unwelcome gripe of jealousy at the thought. There most definitely was not a spare one for Marco. Leah was one of a kind. And it was going to be a killer to do what he knew he needed to do next: regain his distance from her.

Chapter 11

This, thought Leah, shuffling into her new black work uniform, was probably going to be a disaster. She had five waiting on staff. Two assistants in the kitchen. Champagne she'd selected on ice. And what felt like a gazillion dollars worth of fresh food waiting to be served. The only thing not under complete control was her nerves. They were busy having a glowstick party in her brain.

The last week had passed in a whirl. Mrs Cavelli, once she got her own way, was a pussycat of a client, leaving all the food-related decisions to Leah. Presumably she was way too busy bullying sixty people into dumping their existing plans and visiting her for New Year's instead. That and arranging a swing band; a pianist, an ice sculptor and an interior decorator – all at four days' notice at the busiest time of year.

The staff had come from an agency, and were excellent. Almost as good as Lucy and Pip, the girls who worked with Leah at the bistro. Back in her old life; the one she had a million years ago. She really must drop them an e-mail, let them know she was okay – and make that dreaded follow-up phone call to Doug.

Since contacting him to prevent any future unfortunate police related incidents, she'd dodged all his calls. He'd left apologetic message after apologetic message, begging her forgiveness. Not, oddly enough, begging her to come back – but to call him so he could explain himself. Leah suspected Doug had realised what she herself now knew: they'd both had a lucky escape. Maybe he'd realised before she did, and that's why he accidentally screwed the bridesmaid. Or maybe he was just a lech. Who knew?

Stuff had to be sorted with him – there were bank accounts to be closed, her belongings to get shipped, and she owed him at the very least a civil conversation. It took two people to break a relationship as well as make it, and in his own way, he'd been good to her. Minor blip on the wedding day, but years of companionship and kindness before that.

Still. Her first professional catering job in Chicago seemed to be a good enough reason to shirk Doug for the time being. In fact, it was helping her shirk all kinds of things. Like thinking about the fact that Rob, despite living in the same building, hadn't spared her so much as a full sentence in the past three days. It was like he was on a word ration, and if he gave her too many, there'd be a national shortage.

And despite being busy herself, Leah had developed a kind of unintentional radar for his routines. When he'd be coming back up from his office for lunch. When he went for his workouts in the gym. When he finally accepted the working day was over and retreated to his penthouse for a stiff drink. Well, she made that last bit up – she had no idea what he did when he got up there, but after fourteen hours of wheeling and dealing, it seemed a good bet.

In fact, she had the sneaky feeling she was turning into the kind of scary stalker who hid behind potted plants just to catch a glimpse of her target. In fairness that had been just the once, and it was a pretty big potted plant. Rob hadn't even noticed the rustling foliage, he was so distracted.

Shoulders slumped, eyes tired, mouth set in a grim line. It broke her heart to see this new Rob, so careworn and stern. She ached to reach out to him, to massage the stress out of his shoulders, flirt with him 'til he couldn't help but laugh. She yearned to see the old Rob again, to bring back some of the joy and energy they'd shared in Scotland. But he gave her zero encouragement, and treated her with nothing but polite civility. Bearing in mind he was also putting a roof over her head and providing her with a foot in the professional door of catering, she couldn't complain. And yet, it stung. To be so close to him, and unable to capture any of the spark they shared in Scotland. Different world. Different Rob.

Different me, she thought, contorting her arms behind her to snap the buttons on her skirt, smoothing it down over her thighs. She turned to view herself in the full-length mirror. It was almost exactly what she used to wear at the bistro – black pencil, black blouse. But with higher heels and more cleavage. Shiny hair, loads of slap, big fake smile under the bright red lippy.

Almost as though she was trying to impress someone, her conscience whispered. Someone who'd morphed into a harsh-faced businessman with a phone permanently glued to his ear; a frown permanently scarring his forehead, and no time at all for idle chat with the hired help.

She pulled a face at herself in the mirror. She was pathetic. She missed Rob more after a few days with him than Doug after several years.

Luckily, she hadn't had much time for moping. The kitchens in the basement of Cavelli Tower had become her new domain, and that was one change she was thrilled about. She couldn't have asked for better equipment, or a better brief – unlimited budget, no need to turn a profit, and free reign to plan the menu. Dorothea was paying her what she suspected was way above the going rate for caterers, most of which she planned to give back to Rob, whether he wanted it or not. It was something she needed to do, for herself.

And tonight would also be a great showcase for her, in front of a bunch of wealthy and influential potential clients. Cavelli Inc., it turned out, didn't buy and sell reindeer at all. It bought and sold property, and invested in manufacturing and retail. The business had been started by Rob's grandfather, who began importing olives and olive oil from Italy not long after he'd settled in Chicago.

He'd spotted a market that worked, and grew it – starting off by supplying the Italian émigrés living in the city; the restaurants that served them, then expanding into the fine food market. From there he'd invested in some of the businesses he sold to, and the rest was Cavelli family history. His son, Paolo, had taken the company to the next level, and when he died of a heart attack eight years earlier, Rob took over.

According to Dorothea, he'd almost worked himself to death since then, advancing the Cavelli name even further. She didn't say it out loud, but it was obvious she was worried her son was setting himself up to follow in his father's footsteps in more ways than one. Since she'd seen workaholic Rob first-hand in the last few days, Leah thought she might be right.

She wondered, but didn't ask, about the wife. About the wedding ring. About the incident that had left him so broken and bruised. It was none of her business. She would remain as distant and professional as Rob deemed appropriate. And she knew that if she'd asked Dorothea, she'd grass her up, and blow all of her attempts to honour the space he seemed to want between them.

Yeah, right, she thought. Distant and professional. Respectful of personal space. That's you, Leah Harvey. That's why you're wearing perfume seductive enough to make the whole smoked salmon on the slab sit up and whistle, and have enough cleavage on show to make a hooker blush. She pulled the front of her top up a few inches. Maybe it was too much... It was definitely too much. Her chest looked like dessert; two rosy blancmanges popping out to say hello. Another tug. A bit more covered. There. Perfectly respect-able…Assuming you were a lap dancer.

She had no time for wardrobe changes now, it would have to do. Rob probably wouldn't even notice she existed, never mind what she was wearing. She needed to get down to the kitchens. Guests would be arriving in a couple of hours, and there were last minute preparations to be made. Herbs to be sprinkled. Cream to be whipped. Bread to be warmed. Several double vodkas to be downed in one.

Leah grabbed her bag, and took the elevator down to the basement. The kitchens were next to the staff recreation room, a huge hall packed with all kinds of toys. Table football. Video games. Gym equipment. And a full sized sports court for those occasions when a working day wouldn't be complete without chucking a ball around.

As she passed, she heard the sound of scuffling feet squeaking on the shiny floor; of a bouncing ball, and familiar male laughter. It was the first time she'd ever heard the place being used, as most staff were still on their Christmas break. Knowing she could be about to kill the kitty, Leah pushed the door slightly to take a peek.

Inside were Rob and Marco. She was no expert, but they appeared to be playing basketball. Rob had the ball, and was bouncing it in front of Marco, laughing and dodging his attempts to grab it from him. He gave it a final bounce and faked a move to the left. Marco lunged, missed, and fell to the floor. Rob leapt up, shoved the ball through the hoop, landed nimbly on his sneakered feet.

His jogging pants were riding low on his hips; with a delectable arrow of soft black hair pointing downwards over his flat stomach. His chest was bare, golden skin covered in a light sheen, muscles taut and defined and gleaming as he did a mock victory dance around a grumbling Marco. Biceps pumped, abs standing proud, hair damp and curling around his face.

Oh. My. God. I may have an orgasm on the spot just from looking, thought Leah, making a small squeaking sound in the back of her throat. Rob glanced up at her just in time to see the swing doors fall back and hit her on the bum, forcing her to stumble a couple weak-kneed bunny-hops forward, further into the room. And with no potted plants to hide behind, she had no choice but to walk towards them.

The other Cavelli twin wasn't wearing a T-shirt either, she

noticed, but it wasn't possible to look at him for more than two seconds, not when Rob was in the room. Her eyes were devouring every inch of the bronzed muscle on show; wondering if it would be over-stepping the 'just friends' role to lean forward and lick it? All of the feelings she'd been trying to restrain, all of the memories of their naked time together, burst free in a glorious rush of lust. Jesus. How could she ever expect to forget him?

Marco nodded his hellos as he stood up, dusting himself down after his tumble. He looked on, pondering the fact that he hadn't even registered on her radar. That, he thought, ain't the reaction I usually get when semi-naked in the company of women.

Marco realised that he was now invisible to both Leah and Rob. Their body language was giving off so much heat the aircon was going to kick up a notch, and he could almost see the sparks leaping between them. Rob was staring down at her, trying really hard to keep his eyes on her face and away from her cleavage, and Leah was gazing at him with... Hell. Complete and utter adoration. It was the only word that came close to describing what he saw in those pretty eyes of hers.

"How are you, Rob?" Leah asked tentatively. She suddenly felt way too hot and tarty in her uniform. Way too everything.

Rob was covered in a light sheen of freshly-earned sweat, and looked tastier than the entire buffet waiting next door. But his eyes were guarded, closed off, and that familiar frown was back in place. Minutes ago, as she'd looked on from the doorway, he'd been laughing, carefree. Now, with one word from her, poof - happy Rob went bye-bye. Replaced with Robo Rob, the sternest man in town.

At least that's how it felt to her, as she watched his face carefully re-arrange itself. Okay, yes, he'd noticed the boobs – passing Russian space satellites had probably noticed them in this top – but that was just a flash, a quick look before the shut down. Now he was tense, withdrawn. No entry, yet again.

"I'm good," he answered curtly, moving away from her, bouncing the basketball as though he couldn't wait to get back to his game.

He turned his back on her, aimed at the hoop and fired. The ball ran lightly around the rim before dropping through the net, hitting the floor with a dull thud. The only sound in the room.

"Did you want anything, Leah? I'm kind of busy right now," he said, still looking in the opposite direction.

"Right. You're busy," she said, to his bare back. "I see that. Busy. Me too. Sorry to bother you. Must go. I have cream to coddle and waiters to whip."

Leah turned, staggering slightly on her heels, and tottered towards the swing doors. She kept her head held high, didn't fall, and best of all, managed to hold back the sound of sobbing as tears streamed over her cheeks. Panda eyes ahoy.

Okay, she thought. If that's the way he's going to play it, so be it. She recognised a super-sized snub when she saw one, and she could deal with it. She'd dealt with worse. I don't need him, she thought. I don't want him. Right now, I don't even like him.

And if that's really the case, then why does my heart feel like it breaks a tiny bit more every time I see him? And how long before it shatters completely?

***

Marco turned back to Rob as Leah beat her unsteady retreat, threatening to tumble right off her sky-high heels. His twin had given up feigning interest in their game, and was rubbing his forehead as though he felt a migraine coming on, which in Marco's opinion served him well and truly right. Rob may have been too busy playing macho basketball hero to notice, but Marco recognised a crying woman when he saw one. What the hell was going on here?

"Well, brother," he said, stabbing Rob on the shoulder with a sharp finger prod, "I hope you're proud of yourself, you bullying piece of crap. That was downright nasty. Since when did your own misery give you the right to be so cruel to someone else? Where do you get off being so freaking rude, and what the hell has she done to deserve that?"

"She was fine! She knows I'm busy! We're...it's...over. It's not like that anymore. We don't owe each other anything."

"She was *not* fine, and you know it! You can say it's over as much as you god-damn please – but it's not, not for her at least. Can't you see the poor girl's falling in love with you?"

"No!" snapped Rob, throwing the ball so hard at his twin's chest that the blow staggered him backwards, knocking the wind from his lungs. For the second time in minutes, Marco ended up falling flat on his perfectly sculpted backside.

"She can't be in love with me, Marco — I won't let her be! I'm damaged goods, you know that! Me, turning my back on her. That's not rude – that's me trying to get the hell out of her life. Because she deserves better than me staying in it, messing her whole future up! So screw you and screw your dumb-ass theories!"

He stalked away, kicking at the floor as he left, leaving scuff marks on the polished wood and knocking the swing doors back so hard they almost flew off their hinges.

Right, thought Marco, climbing to his feet yet again. No tension there at all.

***

The rest of the night was such a blur that Leah didn't have time for a post-mortem on her feelings. Although her team was top-notch, and the food superb, keeping on top of it all was a full-time job. It was up to her to make sure the chilled bubbly kept flowing; the canapés kept circulating; the sorbet didn't melt. That the staff got their breaks, and that the chocolate fountain didn't spill onto the white damask table linen. Her check list was never-ending, and right at the top was 'keep calm and carry on'.

There were people everywhere. Dorothea had been right — everyone did come. The party was packed with New Year's Eve revellers, small crowds spilling all over the building, dancing, chatting, comparing diamonds, doing business deals. Whatever it was that upper-crust American socialites got up to for fun. They certainly ate a lot, and drank a lot, and that meant constant demands on her crew.

There was so much to do, in fact, that it was relatively easy to avoid him. Rob. Or Mr Cavelli, as she'd started referring to him in her mind. If it was distant and formal he wanted, he could have it. And stick it where the sun didn't shine.

She'd been hoping their new set up would have stretched to 'friendly' at least. Even without the sex, she'd liked him enough to want that. She'd thought the same was true in reverse, which just went to show how naive she was. He'd enjoyed the bonking, yes. But anything more? Gee, ma'am, thanks but no thanks. Not the mighty Mr Cavelli. He was way too busy being a Very Important Penis to bother with her any more. Too busy bouncing his bloody balls to even share a civil word.

Every time she saw him at the party, she adopted her new defence mechanism: going cross-eyed and squinting. Okay, so some of the guests probably thought she had some tragic facial disfigurement, and carrying trays of champagne flutes while cross-eyed and wearing stilettos was a challenge, but it was better than the alternative – being confronted by the vision of a fully-groomed Rob in a tailor-cut tuxedo.

The one time she got caught unawares, she saw him sitting on a sofa with a rail-thin brunette draped over his lap like a travel blanket. Beautiful, in a starving-model kind of way. Leah quickly crossed her eyes and walked away as carefully as she could. It was none of her business. He could drape whoever he liked over his lap. She'd been his Christmas totty; maybe now he was upgrading to New Year totty and that was the lucky girl. He looked as good as he ever did: no sign at all of any anguish, any lingering regret, any memory of her at all. He'd very efficiently erased it all and was clearly busy getting on with his life.

Leah felt the sharp prick of tears welling up, and gestured for another member of the wait staff to come over and cover the room. That kind of pain she just didn't need, especially as the big moment was almost upon them. Five minutes to midnight, and the start of the New Year. She absolutely refused to start it crying over a man. That was just too tragic to contemplate.

She looked around. Everyone seemed to have a glass of something bubbly. The food was mainly eaten, and plates were being discreetly tidied away. There'd be the countdown, the big toast, some more drinking, and then coffee and imported Belgian chocolates all round. It was almost over, and it had gone well. Professionally at least. The Cavellis were obviously big news in this city, and Dorothea spent the night introducing her as their latest 'discovery'. It was a great start to her working life, to her new adventure, and one day she'd be glad of it. One day, when she wasn't an emotional cripple.

Deciding that everything was under control and that she could afford to take a break, Leah edged outside, through the French doors and onto the balcony. The frigid night air attacked her skin until it puckered with goosebumps, and her teeth started to chatter. But it was quiet, and deserted, and she was alone. An over-flowing ashtray showed that it had been the smokers' haunt for the evening, but right now, even they were inside, waiting to celebrate the start of the New Year.

Leah leaned against the chill metal of the railing and looked out over the city: an endless vista of twinkling silver and gold, shining from thousands of windows in hundreds of buildings. The skyscrapers were beacons of light, their reflections dancing like spirits over the river; further out, she could see sparkling trails of colour stretching out into the water at Navy Pier. It was beautiful, like some man-made heaven laid out before her. A city of millions, celebrating, partying, hoping.

Everyone inside Cavelli Tower was excited, hyped with the thrill of starting a new year. Even the staff felt the buzz. And, she realised, everyone at home – or England, at least – was already sleeping it off, six hours ahead. It was early morning there, and Doug was starting a whole new year without her. It would still be dark, with the first grey light of dawn starting to filter through onto the London streets. Trafalgar Square would have its own hangover, and all across the city, people would be crashed out, sleeping, with bits of party popper stuck in their hair.

She wondered what Doug was doing; whether he was missing her, or whether he was with Becky. Whether he'd been working in the bistro that night, or given himself the time off. The year before they'd opened, had a very busy ball of a time with their regulars, but this year was supposed to have been different. They should both be sunning themselves in the Caribbean right now, but life had kind of snuck up on them. She resolved to call him the day after and wish him all the best. Life was too bloody short for bitterness, she knew.

She shivered, realising that life would be even shorter if she stayed out here in sub-zero temperatures for much longer. She needed a coat at least; possibly a balaclava. The snowfall had been heavy since she'd arrived, but Chicago seemed so much better geared up for it than the UK. Nothing stopped. Roads were cleared by giant snow trucks; people carried on walking their dogs and going to work and drinking in bars. They just did it all wearing thermal undies and snow boots. And now here she was, typical Brit idiot, standing out in the dark and the cold at midnight, feeling her eyelashes freeze together like they'd been Superglued.

She heard the doors slide open behind her, and the sound of a raucous countdown spilled out into the night: Nine. Eight. Seven... Just as quickly it was shut off as the door closed again, like someone had switched an overly-loud TV onto mute. Leah anticipated a request for a champagne top up or a decaff non-fat latte or some such, and fixed a large smile on her face. Nobody liked a moody waitress. Unless you were in Paris, of course, where it got you bigger tips.

"You're going to freeze out here, you British idiot," he said, holding out a black coat and draping it over her shoulders. Rob. Of course.

"Ha! Don't call me that – even if I was just thinking it." She replied; glad of the warmth of the cashmere on her skin, but not so sure about the company. After carrying out a successful avoidance manoeuvre all night, she was now trapped. Nowhere to go, unless she fancied taking a plunge off the balcony.

He glanced at his watch, then looked up and pointed out over the city, like he was about to start conducting music. Exactly as he did it, the sky exploded into a riot of colour: purples, greens, golds, reds, all squealing and shimmering in a spectacular fireworks display. It was coming from pontoons set up on the water; from the shores of Lake Michigan; from the parks; from the tops of the tower blocks around them. From everywhere. Further away out in the suburbs, smaller displays erupted, showers of metallic glory falling over the city like shining confetti.

Leah's eyes widened in delight as the whole horizon was suddenly ablaze, swamped with glitter. Noise erupted from everywhere at once: claxons, hooters, car horns, bells, and singing. Shouting and yelling and cheering, from inside, from the streets below, even from the water, as boat parties celebrated the chiming of the hour. It was unbelievable. Leah had never seen anything quite like it, and felt a surge of emotion rush to the surface.

"Happy New Year, Leah," Rob said, leaning close to brush a chaste kiss against her cheek. A cheek that was suddenly wet with tears.

"Are you crying?" he asked, running his fingers over her cheekbones to confirm it. Damn it, he thought, realising that there was every possibility that Marco had been right. He was behaving cruelly, and he had no excuse. This was exactly what he'd been worried about. His blood ran with poison, and now he'd spread it to Leah.

"It's okay," she said, brushing his hand away. Leah was fighting the urge to grab it, to kiss it, to hold it so tight his fingers lost all circulation. But she didn't. Because this was a New Year, and a New Her, and she would not allow herself to feel this way. "It's not your fault, Rob. Ignore me, I'm just being a girl. It's all so beautiful. And, well, I always get a bit weepy on big occasions. Happy New Year to you as well. What are you doing out here anyway?"

Rob gazed at her warily, buying a few moments of time. He knew she was still upset, and every male instinct he had told him to grab this woman close to him, to shield her and protect her and stop those god-damned tears spilling out of her amber eyes. Eyes so large and so moist that he could see every dazzling firework explosion reflected in them. But he held back – he couldn't play with her emotions like that; couldn't blow hot and cold as and when he felt like it.

"My spider senses started tingling," he said, keeping his distance. "I knew that somewhere out here in the big city, Leah Harvey was starting to freeze and turn blue. And it seems to be my mission in life to save you from this crazed hypothermia-related death wish of yours."

In reality, he admitted to himself, it wasn't so much spider senses as plain old eyesight. He'd been watching her all night, radar beeping whenever she was close, trying to ignore the attentions of a very determined Amanda He'd seen the look on Leah's face as she snuck outside: a mix of sadness and loneliness he knew he was at least partially responsible for. He'd invited her here, into his world, his life, and now he couldn't cope with it. It wasn't her fault he got a hard-on whenever he saw her, that he was too screwed up to feel a wave of pleasure without being drowned in guilt. She just didn't understand.

Leah pulled the coat tight around her shoulders. It smelled of his aftershave, and it moved her immediately. She was trying hard not to bury her face in the collar and sniff like a bloodhound. Instead, she smiled up at him and said: "I know. I must have been a penguin in a previous life. Anyway, thanks for the coat. I haven't been able to feel my nose for the last five minutes and I'd look really weird if it dropped off. Better get back inside."

She started to walk by him, back towards the doors. He reached out, grabbed her arm to stop her. He might not be able to give her a relationship, he thought, but he could at least give her an explanation.

"Leah, wait a minute... I wanted to apologise. For earlier. I was rude, and I know I hurt your feelings."

"No! Don't be silly. It's all fine. Anyway – that's last year's news!"

She tried to shake her arm free; he kept hold. If he let her, she'd bolt for the door like a rabbit, he knew. Leah looked down at his hand wrapped around her elbow, but stopped struggling, staring up at him with eyebrows raised.

"It's not fine," he said, feeling a whisper of exasperation at her constant attempts to appear lighthearted when she was obviously in pain. Whether it was his fault, or her ex-fiancé's, or the death of her parents, he didn't know. But she was hurting, and pretending very hard not to be.

She shook her head, fine tendrils of blonde hair haloing around her face. "It *is* fine, and apologies are really not necessary. I was way too busy ogling you with your top off to get my feelings hurt, anyway. I barely heard a word you said."

She smiled up at him – a big, gorgeous…completely phony smile – and tried to pull away from him once more, making for the door. For escape.

"Leah, stop that!" he said, louder than he intended. He tugged her even closer towards him, snapping his arms around her waist so she was pressed tight into his body, face thudding lightly into his chest. He saw a flicker of fear in her shining eyes, and cursed himself for liking it. Way to go, Rob – congratulations, you're stronger than a five foot tall woman.

Leah shoved her hands hard against his chest, buying back a few inches of space. She was angry now, and he really couldn't blame her. He'd been slapped for less than this before, and anticipated the stinging tingle of fingers making contact with his cheek.

It didn't happen. She just went very still, and stared up at him, eyes popping with fury.

"What?" she snapped back. "Stop *what*? What exactly is it I do to upset you so much, Rob? Exist? Shall I take a dive off the balcony just to make your life more peaceful? Go back to England? Join a convent? What is it you want me to stop doing?"

He drew a deep breath, felt the icy air rasp painfully into his lungs. Heard the continued chorus of Auld Lang Syne floating discordantly from inside the building. Looked down at Leah's face, so close to his. Eyes blazing, hair golden, body warm and soft against him. All he had to do was lean down and lay his lips over hers, and maybe he could change everything. Like a charming prince in a fairy tale. Except this was the real world, his world. And happy ever after was a big fat lie.

"Stop trying to defuse me," he said finally, clenching his fists into tight balls so he wouldn't reach out and stroke her face "Stop trying to keep the mood light. Stop trying to excuse my appalling behaviour. Stop trying to cheer me up. Stop ignoring your own feelings when I can see them there, in your eyes. You made me happy at Christmas, Leah, for the first time in years. You distracted me, and laughed with me, and made love with me. And damn, it felt good. But I don't deserve to feel good, Leah. Not then, not now, not ever."

There was a pause. He saw her drinking in his words, felt them quell her own anger like running water on flame. Prepared himself for the question he knew would come next.

"Why?" she asked quietly, her voice a bare whisper above the sounds of the city's celebration. He saw, rather than felt, the gentle play of her cold fingertips along his jaw; the sweet warm cloud of her breath hanging in the chill air between their faces. He couldn't bear it. Couldn't bear to have her touch him. To have anyone touch him, really touch him, ever again.

"Why don't you deserve to feel good, Rob? Tell me why."

He pulled her hand roughly away from his face, forcing it back down to her side and holding it there. She needed to stay away from him. He was toxic, and always would be.

"Because Christmas is when I killed them, Leah. When I killed my wife, and our baby."

Chapter 12

As soon as the words were out, forced from between gritted teeth, Rob shoved her away, leaving the coat behind and storming back into the building. Leah stood still, so shocked she couldn't even go after him. The pain in those words; etched on to his face, had been so intense. The kind of pain that had eaten deep into his soul, changing the very essence of who he was. Of who he could ever be. She had no idea what had happened to his wife and his baby, but she knew without a shadow of doubt that guilt had replaced everything else in his heart: all love, all happiness, all hope.

She understood that kind of guilt. She'd lived with it herself for years, since her parents' death. Survivor's guilt, her therapist had called it. But what the therapist had never understood was that it was more than just guilt at surviving – it was because of her they were even in that hotel in the first place. She'd practically kicked them out of the house so she could have a 'grown up' 18th birthday party with friends from catering college, and the boy she'd been seeing for a few months, David. She liked him, and she was sick of being a virgin – so that, she'd decided, was the night. She had the condoms. She'd read the Cosmo sex survey. She was going to become a woman. And for that, she needed her parents very much out of the house.

They'd agreed, of course. They'd trusted her, loved her. Gone

97

away to the coast for the night to give her the freedom she craved. And they never came back.

So yeah, she understood guilt. The kind of guilt that twisted you around inside until you were someone completely new. And until recently, she'd have said she lived with it as well as she could, building a decent life for herself despite being orphaned at eighteen. But now she knew differently. Now she recognised the lies she'd told herself. She'd moved from one set of parents to Doug, who was older, wiser, more settled. Was it any surprise at all that it hadn't worked out?

They were like a pair of cripples, her and Rob. Staggering through their lives, bowed down by invisible burdens. Maybe they could help each other. If only he'd let her try.

She screwed the coat tighter around her, feeling tears work their icy way down her cheeks, pooling in her collarbone. She cast up a quick prayer for help: for her, for Rob, for all the broken people out there in the world hoping this New Year would bring them something better than the last.

The door opened again, and her face snapped up, heart thudding as she imagined he'd returned. If he had, she'd react better; she wouldn't stand there gaping like a hungry koi carp, she'd grab him and hold him and refuse to be pushed aside. Make him talk to her whether he wanted to or not.

But it wasn't him. It was Marco, eyes narrowed as they adjusted to the dark. She knew he'd been drinking all night, but he seemed suddenly sober, alert. Strong and concerned. It was a shame it was the wrong man.

"Leah," he said, his face set and serious. "What's wrong with Rob? He came through a minute ago looking like death, and stormed off to his apartment. And now... You look the same. Did something happen with you two?"

"Oh Marco, I don't know. I don't know what to do! He told me – told me that he'd killed his wife and baby. That's not true, is it, Marco? Rob could never hurt someone like that. I know he couldn't. Tell me it's not true."

Marco let out the world's biggest sigh as he closed the doors behind him. She could see his shoulders slump, like someone had let all the air out of him. Funny how one man's guilt, one man's pain, always had a way of spreading. Marco loved his brother, and she could see in the lines of his body, the frown on his face, that he tried to carry some of his burden.

"Of course not. He didn't kill anyone, it was a terrible accident. But they died anyway, and he's convinced it's his fault. He's always blamed himself, and I don't know if that will ever change. When I met you, Leah, I saw the way he looked at you. I hoped, I really did. It was the first time I'd seen him happy since it happened. I know my Mom thought the same – that at last, someone had come along who could shake him out of it. But I was wrong. He'll never change. Maybe... maybe he can't change."

"How? How did they die?" Leah asked, screwing her eyes up tight to stop the flow of tears. Tears that were flowing for Rob, for herself, for his poor wife and baby, lost forever.

"That's his story to tell, Leah," said Marco, an answering gleam of sadness in his own eyes. "He's already told you more than most, but the rest of it? That's up to him."

She nodded, accepted his decision. He was right. If Rob ever wanted to open up, she'd be there for him – but it had to be his choice. She could offer her support, but she couldn't force him to take it.

"Should I go and find him?" she asked. "Will it help if I try and talk to him? Or just be with him, even if he stays silent all night? It kills me to think of him up there on his own, at New Year, feeling like this. Is there anything I can do to help him?"

Marco gazed out at the city below them, thinking carefully about his reply before he spoke.

"Honestly, Leah? Right now, no, I don't think there is. I know how you feel, it's the world we've lived in for years now, me and Mom. Seeing his pain, but not being able to take any of it away.

He won't let us. Won't let anyone stop him punishing himself like this. So no, sweetheart, leave him be, for now at least. He'll drink a bottle of JD, pass out comatose, and wake up tomorrow feeling like a bear with a sore head. Take it from someone who's tried, when he reaches this stage, there's no pulling him back from the abyss. He just jumps right in. It's where he wants to be. Where he needs to be."

Marco looked at her, this tiny, blonde munchkin of a woman, and knew she was feeling a world of pain on his twin's behalf. He knew she'd probably chop off her right hand if it would make Rob feel better. He knew that maybe, just maybe, his screw-up of a brother Rob was right about one thing – she deserved better.

"Come on inside," he said, placing a comforting arm around her shoulder. "We've been here before. Many times. He'll survive until the morning, he always does. And my mother has about a thousand potential business contacts to introduce you to..."

***

Leah was summoned to brunch with the family the next day. After what felt like thirty seconds of sleep, she was only glad she didn't have to cook it as well. She was drained on every level, and didn't even feel capable of opening a box of Cornflakes. There were dark circles under her eyes that even Touché Éclat wasn't touche-ing, and every step she took felt like she was dragging Ugg boots through sand. It wasn't only the emotional over-drive, it was the sleep deprivation.

She'd been up until about four in the morning helping with the clear up, trying to keep her mind off the real problem. When she'd finally collapsed into bed, she'd lain awake for hours, staring at the ceiling and replaying that scene on the balcony over and over in her mind. Wondering if she could have done anything differently, anything better. Anything to keep Rob from jumping head first into that abyss of his.

The end result of her anguished night stared back at her from the bathroom mirror: Bride of Frankenstein, on a bad hair day.

In comparison, Mrs Cavelli was sitting erect at the dining table, make-up perfect, not a white-grey hair out of place. Marco was slouched next to her, more rumpled, spreading jam onto a croissant. He gave Leah a wink as she sat down, and she managed a weak smile in return. Rob was opposite her, eyes red-rimmed and sore, stubble turning into something more serious, hair sticking out at finger-in-socket angles. There was a copy of the Wall Street Journal spread out on the table in front of him, which he was studying intently. No food, just a drained glass of orange juice. Looked like Marco's predictions had been bang on. The bear did indeed have a sore head, and he looked even crappier than her.

Rob didn't so much as acknowledge her arrival into the room, and Leah felt the stirrings of an urge to poke the bear with a big stick. Welcome to the New Year, she thought, Rob Cavelli style. From life-changing revelations on the strike of midnight to being ignored over Danish pastries, all in a matter of hours.

"Good morning, Rob," she said, as she pulled her chair in under the table. He nodded vaguely in her direction, swiped at his crusted eyes, and stayed silent.

"Enjoying the paper?" she asked, looking down at the Journal that was taking up half the table.

"Yeah," he said, not even looking up to meet her gaze.

She nodded, looked down at the paper again, and replied: "Good. Do you find you get more from the stock tips when you read them upside down?"

Marco sniggered, and Mrs Cavelli studiously nibbled the corner of a pain au chocolat. Rob glared at them, picked up the rustling newspaper, and switched it around until it was the right way up.

"Better?" Leah asked, pouring herself a coffee.

"Yeah," he mumbled. It was obviously his word for the day, and as much as she was going to get out of him. Served her right for bear-baiting. She should have left him alone, let him have the space and silence he craved, but heck, she was tired too. Tired of sleepless nights. Tired of wondering what was going on in his mind. Tired of wanting to hold him, to comfort him, and not being able to. Tired of him pushing her away. In Scotland she'd struggled to keep her hands off him for sexual reasons; here, now, it was more. It was a basic instinct to reach out to another human being, and fighting it all the time was getting pretty exhausting.

"So, Leah," said Dorothea, shaking a napkin onto her lap and attracting the attention of everyone in the room. "I thought it went amazingly well last night – you did an outstanding job! Everyone was full of compliments, and I simply lost track of the amount of guests who asked for your details. Isn't she fantastic, boys?"

"Truly fantastic," said Marco, mumbling around a mouthful of food, "you did well, Leah, really well."

Rob remained silent, until his mother appeared to kick him in the shin under the table. With a pair of very pointy shoes.

"Ouch. Yeah. She's amazing," he replied dutifully, making it sound like the rote answers primary school kids give in assembly. If it hadn't been for his obvious distress, Leah would probably have considered kicking him under the table herself.

Mrs Cavelli was staring at him the way a butterfly collector might at a particularly impressive specimen of Red Admiral. Like he was a thing of great beauty that she admired, but was about to stick a spike through. There was a slight shake of her head, a flutter of sadness in the green of her eyes, then she turned her glance back to Leah. Rob returned to his paper, oblivious to the tensions swirling around him. Oblivious, or just too hungover to care.

"Well, it wasn't just the food that was a hit, Leah," Dorothea said, "it was you personally. I know you're fresh out of a relationship—"

"So fresh, in fact, I was still wearing the wedding dress a few days ago," Leah replied, not liking the sound of this particular conversation, or the scheming look on Mrs Cavelli's face.

"Yes, so I understand. But that's the past, and this is the present, and you have a future to think of. Heaven forbid anyone ever tells me the details of what you and my son got up to in Scotland – some things are not meant for a mother's ears – but I believe that as of now, you are young, free and single. Is that right?"

"Yeah," answered Rob on her behalf, his voice gruff and definite.

Leah picked up a bread roll from the basket and pinged it at the side of his head. It bounced off, leaving fresh crumbs in his already unruly hair. He grimaced, like Thor's hammer had smashed into his skull.

"You shut up, sunshine," she said. "I can speak for myself. Dorothea, yes, technically you are correct, but I am *really* not interested in men at the moment. Any of them. I have work to establish, I have to sort out my finances, find somewhere to live—"

"Oh piffle!" she interrupted, dismissing Leah's to-do list in the way only a wealthy woman could. "That's all very dull. Listen, last night, I promised Rick Machin I'd ask if he could have your phone number. Rick Machin, my dear, is one of the most eligible bachelors in all of Chicago. Probably third most eligible, after the two specimens sitting at the table with us right now."

Marco snorted in amusement, but didn't speak. Rob, Leah thought, frowned a little bit harder, but it was tough to tell with his face almost slumped into the newsprint. She turned back to Dorothea, who was waiting intently for her reaction.

"No," Leah replied, thinking it best to keep it simple. She'd seen Mrs Cavelli in action before, and being subtle was like an earthworm trying to reason with an oncoming steamroller, just before the squelch. "No, you can't give him my phone number."

"No? What do you mean, no? Why ever not? He's handsome, charming, a splendid chef..."

"*No*," Leah repeated, stressing the word as firmly as she could without shouting.

"But darling, you'd have so much in common!"

"We'd have nothing in common, and I'm not interested. I'm very grateful for the opportunity you gave me last night, Mrs Cavelli, but if you carry on trying to bully me into this, I'm afraid you're next in line for a bread roll to the head."

There was a deathly silence. Marco held his hands over his mouth to stop himself from laughing out loud, and even Rob's lips twitched in that familiar sideways half-smile she already knew so well. The half-smile she hadn't seen much of at all since they came to Chicago. He looked up from the paper and caught her staring. The smile disappeared. Whatever he saw in her face was enough to turn his gaze cold, like the lights had been switched off inside him.

There was a beat as they locked stares, all humour drained from the situation. His eyes were deep, dark, angry. Angry with her? With himself? With everything? Leah desperately wanted to look away from that icy glare but somehow couldn't, and she felt a fierce blush burning up over her neck and cheeks.

"No, Mom's right, Leah," he said after several long, cool seconds. "You should give it a go. Rick's a nice guy — I never met a woman yet who didn't think so. Go out on a date. Have some fun. It'll be good for you. Maybe you need to start over, get away from your bad decisions. All of them."

The tension in the room ratcheted up a notch, as Marco and Dorothea looked on. It was clear to Leah that he included himself in the 'bad decisions' category, and her heart ached for him. There had been hints of this side of him in Scotland, but here in this room, with what seemed to be the physical and emotional hangover from hell, it was in full force: he hated himself with a raging intensity that excluded everything but his own pain and guilt.

Leah had no idea if that kind of hatred could be overcome, and suspected she'd never find out – she couldn't help a man who didn't want to be helped. Who didn't even want her around. He seemed desperate to offload her onto someone else, onto this Rick Machin character, to get rid of her. Maybe he wanted to wash his hands of even partial responsibility for her, wipe the slate clean, pretend nothing had ever happened between them. It hurt, but perhaps he was right, and she did need to start over. Because the

Rob sitting in front of her was nothing like the man she'd spent her Christmas with. He was twisted, and sad, and humourless, and verging on cruel. Her heart might be tugging the rest of her towards him, but her survival instinct told her to slow right down.

"You really think I should?" she asked. Her tone was neutral; her face was neutral. Her heart was thudding like a wild thing in her chest. She felt furious and hurt and insulted and confused, all at the same time – but fought like a wild thing to keep all of those emotions hidden.

Rob shrugged his broad shoulders, pulled a 'who-gives-a-damn' face, and said one word:

"Yeah."

The word of the day.

Leah stood up, no longer able to bear being in the same room as him. She paused in the doorway, looked over her shoulder.

"You know what, Dorothea? Why not? Give him my number. Maybe it's time I had a little fun of my own."

Chapter 13

She didn't speak to Rob again for almost a fortnight. It was a long fortnight, and a strange one, made up of what felt like a thousand days and nights and a million ups and downs. She felt abandoned, and lonely, and strangely determined to try and break through to him.

He'd left for New York three days after their laugh-a-minute brunch, and had been a ghost in the time in between. He spent eighteen hours a day in his office, and did a spectacular job of avoiding her and everyone else when he was at home; evading them all with manoeuvres worthy of a special-ops unit.

Leah had given them both a day to cool down, then did what came naturally to her: tried to make things better. Rob had made it obvious he didn't want a relationship with her — but he clearly needed a friend, whether he realised it or not. She'd seen it now, the depth of his pain; the black hole of despair that lived inside him, consuming him like an emotional tapeworm. Nobody deserved that, no matter how much they blamed themselves for the death of those they loved. Not even you, a tiny voice reminded her; not even you.

Rob had no idea that she could understand his anguish in a way his family couldn't, that her guilt parade was right up there marching in time with his. She owed it to both of them to reach out one last time, she decided. To try and break through those layers of despair and self-loathing, even if it meant risking rejection on all kinds of levels. It – he – was worth it.

Rob, however, had other ideas. He turned into the Invisible Man, separating himself from her and his family like a plague victim. She was forced to try and communicate the way any 21st century woman did: by text, voicemail, and online. Even if he wasn't around to physically talk to, there were plenty of other ways to harass someone in the modern era, she knew.

The flipside of that, Leah soon discovered, was that there were also plenty of ways to be ignored. The texts went unanswered. His PA Felicia repeatedly informed her, in tones that escalated from sympathetic to annoyed, that he was unavailable. She'd obviously decided that Leah was made of restraining order material, and heck, maybe she was right. Rob, it seemed, had gone underground. He'd even started staying out all night, presumably in a hotel, to avoid them all.

His silence made her feel like an obsessed teenager breaking every girl rule in the book, but her ego could take a few dents, she decided. There was more at stake here than protecting her pride.

Leah had the strongest feeling that if she didn't manage to break through Rob's barriers now, it would be too late. He'd spend the rest of his days closed off and half alive, forever a spectator at the show. And in the same way he'd helped her when fate delivered her shivering and sad to his doorstep, she now needed to help him. Or at least to try. To show him that someone cared enough to see through the arrogance and the bullshit, all the way through to the man inside. The softer, gentler man she couldn't quite give up on. The man who had, at least for a few crazy days over Christmas, been capable of happiness. He'd had it once – and she wasn't ready to accept that he would never have it again. If he'd let her, she'd show him that she understood – and that there were better ways to live than this.

She wasn't pursuing him so she could force him into a

relationship he didn't want. She wasn't pursuing him to get him into bed, no matter how much fun that had been. She was pursuing him because she cared; because she wanted to have one last try at reaching him. One last try at salvaging something from the wreckage of their friendship before she took his advice, and moved on.

In the end, none of it mattered. Rob left for the Big Apple without so much as a goodbye, virtual or otherwise, to either Leah or his family. So much for salvage.

Marco tried to assure her it was Rob being his 'usual beast of a workhorse', but she wasn't stupid. She could tell everyone else was worried about him as well. That Marco and Mrs C were also wondering what he'd do next, and how much damage it would cause him. That this was worse than usual, even by Rob's self-destructive standards.

The silent treatment continued while he was in away in New York. Unless he was in business meetings 24/7, he was still deliberately ignoring her. She checked and rechecked her phone, just in case the battery had accidentally fallen out. She scoured the spam box of her emails, in case roberto@cavelliinc.com had been junked. She even started doing google news searches for him and monitoring the online financial press, on the off chance he was mentioned. It was all together tragic, she knew – but not as tragic as the way Rob was wasting his whole life away.

After four more days of stalker-quality behaviour, Leah sat down in front of her laptop, sighed, and finally closed the lid on both the computer and her hope.

It had been a week since he'd last spoken to her, at brunch on New Year's Day. When his parting shot had been to encourage her to date another man.

A week without contact of any kind. A week of talking into a void. A week of frantically responding to no response at all. Enough was enough; even lunatic optimists needed to know when it was time to give themselves a good talking to. It didn't matter what empathy she felt, or how pure her motives were: Rob didn't want to know. It was time to stop, for the sake of her own mental health. To return to the land of the sane, and to her own life; her own problems. God knew there were enough of them. She'd put everything on hold, and now was the time of reckoning – time to get her own house in order, as Rob clearly wasn't interested in anything she had to say.

It was the only sensible thing to do, but still she felt like a coward. That she was giving up. Giving up on the man she knew he could be; giving up in the way even Marco and Dorothea seemed to have done. They'd accepted his fate, and so had Rob. Why was she the only one crazy enough to still have hope? A hope that now needed to be tied up in a box, and put away in a shelf in the corner of her melting brain.

She was doing the right thing, she told herself. There might be nothing more she could do for him, especially when he wasn't willing to try, but her own life was still a work in progress. She could take the positive change he'd brought about, and move on. Like he kept telling her to do. Leave the bad behind – and Lord knows there was enough of it. Part of her was scared: obsessing about Rob and his emotions had been a handy way of distracting her from her own. From the sneaking suspicion that she'd fallen in love with a man that didn't want her; from the fallout with Doug, from addressing the fact that she found herself here, in a city she didn't know, with her life in very elegant tatters around her.

She had to get a grip.

She spent the next week engaging both her brain and her body in more positive activity, determined to do what Rob very obviously thought she should. Hold her head high, and move forward, to God only knew what.

She started looking seriously for apartments, discovering the online world of Craigslist and leaving the to-let ads in the paper covered in big red circles. She sorted out a bank account, and filled in all the forms Marco had given her for the work visa. She bought a diary, and returned the calls of the potential clients passed on by Dorothea, booking in provisional dates and arranging meetings. She tried to distract herself planning possible menus and sourcing stock and costing up staff. She sat and doodled designs for a website, and made inquiries with printing companies.

She walked, for miles and miles, falling in love with the city. Dawdling at the edges of Lake Michigan; watching people jog around the beachfront paths in seventeen layers of sweats, panting their hot breath in clouds of steam into the icy air. She read, sitting on the wooden benches in Lincoln Park; and travelled backwards and forwards on the 'L', Chicago's answer to the Tube, watching the people and the places. She borrowed a bike, and cycled on the frosty paths along Lakeshore Drive, knuckles white with cold. She found fresh food markets, and tiny restaurants, and public gardens where you could buy cuttings of all kinds of herbs and spices. She stayed as busy as it was possible to be.

And finally, when all of that started to fade, when the blur of activity wasn't enough to dim the memory of Rob's haunted eyes on New Year's Eve, she gave in on one last battle.

She gave in to Dorothea's Give Rick A Chance campaign, and arranged a date. The first proper date she'd been on since she met Doug, five years and a lifetime ago.

She had nothing to lose and Rob, she decided, would probably dance a little jig and sing a cheerful ditty as soon as he found out. Assuming he ever came back to Chicago at all. Maybe, once he discovered that Bunny Boiler Harvey had moved on to a new victim, he'd be on the next flight home, full of relief at his lucky escape.

Even the thought of him being glad to get rid of her drenched her with anguish, tears pricking her eyes as she prepared for her night out. She shook it off, splashed water on her face and stared into the mirror of the bathroom. This was no way to be feeling on date night. Tears and mascara just didn't mix. She grabbed a red lipstick from the vanity, unscrewed the lid, and scrawled on the glass in big block letters: GET A GRIP!

She took a step back, surveyed her crimson creation, and nodded. A motto to live by.

She had a date. With a real life man who was genuinely interested in her. She needed to concentrate on that man tonight, instead of A, the imaginary one who'd flown thousands of miles away to escape her, or B, the fiancé who loved her so much he accidentally bonked her bridesmaid. Rick Machin was C – an unknown quantity who might be just what she needed.

Determined to give the night her very best try, Leah kept the tears at bay, and applied her make-up with extra special care. She straightened her hair so it flowed like a golden river down her back, and paired a slinky navy mini-dress with heels that brought her to the towering height of five foot five. Big hoopy ear-rings. Perfume everywhere. And a final lick of cherryade lip gloss.

There, she thought, surveying her handiwork. Not bad at all. Thank God for make-up and the million and one other tricks girls could hide behind. She may feel like she was shrivelling to dust inside, but she looked great.

Great enough, in fact, that she didn't even feel out of place on the 96th floor of the Hancock Tower, accompanied by Chicago's third most eligible bachelor. They'd had dinner, and now drinks, and the night was going about 200% better than Leah had expected it to. Rick Machin, it turned out, was fabulous company. He was funny, attentive, well-mannered, and a rich source of scurrilous gossip about people she hoped to one day count as clients.

They were drinking Windy City cocktails, and sitting by a floor-to-ceiling window that made Leah feel like she could fall out and tumble through the sky at any minute. Rick, handsome in a cool blonde tennis coach kind of way, was sitting close enough that he could grab hold of her if she did.

"So, why did you ask me out, Rick Machin?" she asked, boldly. This was her third Windy City cocktail, and it was coming pretty close to blowing her over.

Rick grinned, and lots of little creases appeared at the sides of his blue eyes. She liked that in a man. Showed he smiled a lot. He was exceptionally well-dressed, tall, 'dishy', as her mother might have said. Very GQ. Worked as a senior partner at his family's law firm, who represented the Cavellis. He was part of the Chicago elite, which made the question even more relevant in her eyes. She was, after all, only the hired help, and needed to know if she'd be driving home in a pumpkin at midnight.

"That's very direct, Leah – is that a you thing, or an English thing?" he asked.

"Ummm, me, I think. But what I meant was, why ask me out, when I'm told you could have your pick of the gorgeous young things of Chicago. Don't get me wrong, I know I'm okay. But I'm hardly a supermodel, am I?"

"Maybe I'm tired of supermodels," he said, sipping his own cocktail. Non-alcoholic, as he was driving. Somewhere deep inside her slowly pickling brain, Leah knew that was a bad thing – to be drinking this much herself when her companion was sober. It was a slippery slope, and she was wearing very high heels.

"That doesn't sound likely," she replied, placing her glass down on the table so she wouldn't be tempted to start yet another one. "Surely if you're tired of supermodels, you're tired of life?"

"Supermodels aren't all they're cracked up to be," he said. "They don't eat. They don't cook. They don't say 'sodding hell' when they spill olives on their lap. And they don't laugh so hard they snort Windy City Martinis out of their nostrils, either."

"That was your fault," Leah replied. "You shouldn't have made me laugh when I was drinking."

"You've been laughing all night," he pointed out. "And drinking all night. It was inevitable the two would collide at some point or another."

She nodded happily, feeling the warm and fuzzy effect of the alcohol swim down as far as her toes. "You're right. I have laughed a lot tonight. In fact, I've really enjoyed myself."

"You sound surprised. What were you expecting? Dull guy in suit?"

"Well, yes, of course...but also...well, there's stuff. About me. Runaway bride and all that. Plus other stuff. Stuff that's not been very laughter-inducing recently."

"Stuff?" he queried, raising one eyebrow. "That's very articulate. Deep dark secrets?"

Rick reached out and took her hand in his, stroking her fingers, her wrist. It felt nice to be touched, and touched kindly. It felt pleasant, maybe more if she gave it a chance. But there was no shock of excitement. No spark, like there had been with that other guy. The one she wasn't obsessing about tonight. He Who Shall Not Be Named.

Even as the thought crossed her mind, she tensed, and pulled her hand away from Rick's, trying to keep the smile fixed on her face. There might be other men for her, one day. But not Rick, and not now, no matter how many cocktails she downed.

"Not deep and dark, no. Just stuff. Stuff that makes me think maybe I should lock myself up in a cupboard for a few months until I get my head on straight. Look Rick, I really have had great fun tonight, and goodness knows I needed it. Under different circumstances, I'd probably have wrestled you under the table and snogged you by now. I hope we can be friends and do this again, but right now, it can't be anything more than that. I'm just not girlfriend material. Assuming the nostril thing hadn't put you off already."

"No," he said, "it hadn't put me off. In fact I found it weirdly attractive. I may be turning into some kind of pervert."

"You're not one already?" she asked, smiling to take the edge off what they both knew was a rejection.

"Only a little bit," he said, returning her grin, "and only on a full moon. Leah, I had a great night too. And I won't lie, I'd be happier if it ended with you back at my place, discussing my perversions in private. But if you need me to be just a friend, then you've got

113

it. I can do that. And I suppose, if forced, I could always call in the occasional supermodel to fulfil my other needs..."

Leah burst out laughing, luckily with her mouth empty this time. God, it felt good to laugh again. It felt good to flirt, and know it would come to nothing. It felt good to put on make-up and high heels and feel admired. It felt good to spend the night engaged in shallow, harmless fun with another human being. Maybe tonight, with a belly full of booze and nothing more serious than Rick's risqué jokes floating through her mind, she would finally be able to sleep properly.

"That's brilliant," she said, both relieved and relaxed. "Now, friend of mine, could you be a love and take me home? I have the sneaky suspicion I might be a wee bit hammered."

Rick paid the bill, and they left. The night might not be heading in quite the direction he'd hoped, but the smile never faded, and the good humour never waned. Rick, she decided, was just plain easy to be around. If only she fancied him, he'd be the perfect man.

When they arrived back at Cavelli Tower, he offered her a hand to help her out of the car.

"Come on," he said, "I'll escort you to your chambers. Dorothea would have me shot at dawn if you broke an ankle on the way up."

The car was some low-slung sporty affair, and the ground did suddenly feel a bit unsteady beneath her heels, so she took it, grateful of the support.

They rode in the security coded elevator to Leah's floor, and stood outside her door saying their goodbyes. Rick was holding both her hands, and she was still giggling at his latest gag. Something foul involving a pot bellied pig, Elvis Presley and a turkey baster. She genuinely couldn't remember when she'd last laughed so much, at something so stupid. It was like being back in high school again, without the hormones or love hearts on her pencil case.

"So..." he said, as the laughter subsided, squeezing her fingers lightly. "God loves a trier, or so I'm told – any chance of coming in for coffee? Seeing as I'm such a funny guy?"

His face was dressed up in such a plaintive, little-boy expression that she started laughing again. He was indeed a trier, and she wasn't even remotely fooled by the innocent act.

"Not a chance, pal," she replied firmly, unable to stop smiling. "I'm not quite that drunk, and, well, just no. It wouldn't work, Rick, I'm sorry. You're a lovely—"

"Let me guess – I'm a lovely guy and some woman will be lucky to have me? I'm a great catch, but you're not interested in throwing out a line?"

"Wow, it's like you read my mind… But you *are* a great catch, Rick. You already know that. Third most eligible bachelor in Chicago, or so I'm told."

"Third? Ha! I'm insulted – who told you that? And who beat me to first and second?"

"Dorothea Cavelli, and her sons," she replied, smirking slightly. Rick clasped his hands to his chest, as though he'd been stabbed in the heart.

"Damn that biased bitch. Well, you can't blame me for trying, Leah. I had a great time tonight, and I really do think you're gorgeous. Now, as you've managed to do the unthinkable and resist my charms all evening, I can only conclude that there's someone else on the scene. Someone too stupid to realise what he's got. So remember I'm only a phone call away. I could always help with guy tactics."

"Thanks, Rick. That's very kind, but I don't think there's any point. I don't think he even likes me, never mind anything more than that."

"Then he's an idiot," Rick replied, "and if you ever reveal his secret identity, I'll tell him so myself, after I've kicked his ass for making you look so sad. Anyway, sweetheart, as you're insisting on going to bed alone, I'll leave you to it. I'd recommend drinking a large glass of water first, and having several Advil ready to go in the morning. But before I leave, Leah, I'm going to kiss you goodnight. Just to see if we can't chase him out of your head for a minute or two. Don't argue – you might even like it!"

He smiled and leaned forward, taking her gently in his arms. His movements were cautious, his touch soft, his eyes alert on hers. Like he was moving slowly for her sake, giving her all the time in the world to protest if she wanted to, looking for any sign that she was distressed. Being a man, but being nice about it.

She wasn't distressed; in fact now he'd raised the issue, she was curious. She let him embrace her, wondering if he was right. If his kiss could chase Rob out of her head. If it would rock her world and bring her to her knees in a frenzy of sexual desire. If kissing Rick would exorcise the ghost of kisses past. It was worth a go.

She turned her face up towards his; relaxed into his arms. Rick needed no further encouragement, and leaned down to kiss her.

Leah responded as enthusiastically as she could, winding her fingers into his blonde hair, snuggling close to the long line of his body. She tried to loosen up, to give herself over to it. To really, truly enjoy it. She gave it her best shot, but she still knew the answers pretty much straight away. Nothing was rocking, apart from her on her tipsy heels. Rob was still very much there, a glowering black cloud lodged in her mind, just like he always was. The touch of Rick's lips was pleasant, but nothing more.

He pulled away after the kiss, keeping her in his arms, hands clasped low on her back, looking down at her upturned face.

"Anything?" he said, his tone making it a question.

"Nothing," she replied, shaking her head sadly.

"Damn!" he answered through gritted teeth. "I've lost my mojo! I need to find me a supermodel and get some practice… Goodnight, Leah. I'll see you soon, friend."

She couldn't help but giggle as he turned to leave, giving her a cheery wave. She hadn't dented his ego after all. She suspected it was made of titanium. That was a good thing — Rick was the first non-Cavelli friend she'd made in Chicago, and she didn't want to lose him this quickly. And despite the fact that Rob seemed to have ruined her for all other men on the kissing front, she felt a seed of happiness for the first time in days.

Well, not happiness exactly she thought, fumbling with the key to her apartment. But something slightly less than abject misery. She was still smiling as she finally managed to crack the Da Vinci code and get the door open, tripping over her own feet slightly on the way in.

***

Thank God, thought Rob, hidden behind the fire exit, door cracked open a couple of inches while he watched. He released the breath he'd been holding for what felt like hours, moved his feet to get some blood flowing back through his calves.

He'd been hidden there for the entire farewell scene, immobile and silent. Not spying, he told himself. Protecting her interests. She was vulnerable right now, and he was doing the honourable thing and looking out for her. Rob recognised the lie as soon as he thought it: there was nothing honourable about the way he felt. The fact that he wanted to follow Rick Machin down into the parking lot and beat the crap out of him proved that.

But at least she was in, and she was in alone. For a moment there he thought Rick was going to push for the invite, despite the fact that Leah was obviously drunk. And what would he have done then? Called the cops? Faked a fire alarm? He had no right to stop her from doing what any grown woman might have the urge to do from time to time: get naked with an attractive man.

There was a pounding sensation pulsing through his veins, hammering at his temples and jaw. He thought it might be his own blood literally boiling at the thought. He flexed his fingers, grimaced as he did it – he'd been clenching his fists so tightly he'd cut half-crescent shapes into his own palms. It had been the only way to stay quiet as he watched Rick Machin put his grubby paws all over Leah. He'd been too far away to hear a word they were saying, but the visual was enough, thank you very much.

He'd got back from New York that afternoon, feeling calmer and more in control. With a plan of action. A to-do list that would put his life back on the path it had been on before Christmas. Before her. And now, a few short hours later, he was hiding in the stairwell of his own building, acting like a Peeping Tom and self-harming. That was the effect Leah had on him. And that was why she had to go.

The trip to New York had been good. Good for business, good for him. As ever, the guilt about Meredith had needed to run its course. It was like a river: if you tried to dam it up, it always came out somewhere, flooding the levee when you least wanted it to. So he'd run – away from Marco's cloying concern and Dorothea's transparent attempts to make him jealous. Away from the complexities of living under the same roof with a group of people who all thought they could fix him.

Mainly, he'd run away from Leah. He'd ignored the texts, the messages. The silly email with its smiley faces. The flow of irate memos from Felicia. Ignored everything she'd sent him, on the principle that if he did it long enough, even Leah would give up on him. He'd tried to put her off with the brutal truth on New Year's, and when that hadn't worked, hoped absence would do it. Absence, and arrogance. Two of his specialist subjects.

He'd come home to face her. To explain that he had some kind of incurable disease that made him a bad man to be around. That turned him into an unremitting ass. To help her househunt, help her arrange her next client, nag Marco about the visa – whatever the hell it took to get her out of the building. Out of eyeshot. Out of his bloodstream. He needed her gone, and would try to do it with as much kindness as he could. After all, it has was his crazy, spontaneous, sexed-up offer that had landed her here in the first place.

Because no matter what he'd thought originally, they could never just be friends. Sure, he believed her when she said she wanted to try. And maybe she was nobler than him; maybe she could control her libido long enough for them to be close. But he damn well couldn't. He'd never be able to look at her without remembering the feel of her soft curves beneath him; to listen to her voice without recalling the moans and sighs she made as she climaxed. To see her in clothes and fail to imagine her without them. He couldn't be her friend – but he could try not to be her enemy. The least he owed her was civility as he shoved her out the door.

When Leah hadn't even been at home when he got back, he'd felt deflated. And, as he stared at the closed door to her apartment wondering where she was and what she was doing, self-aware enough to recognise his own arrogance: did he expect her to be sitting on the doorstep like a puppy, waiting for her master's return? She was an adult. She had a life. He'd positively encouraged her to go out and get one, last time they'd spoken. Could he blame her if that was what she'd done? Even Leah's goodwill had its limits.

That was fine, he told himself through gritted teeth. That was what he wanted too. And it was no big deal – he would see her later, or the next day. Whatever she was out doing, he was okay with it. It was all good. He was good... Everything was cool.

Except that by the time it reached 11pm, the cool had turned into more of a cold sweat. He was tired, and should have been in bed, but something kept him up, awake, developing callouses from hitting redial on his phone.

She didn't have a car, so someone else was driving her. Neither Marco nor his mother were taking calls either, so she might be with them. Even Artie had no idea where she was, which was like God admitting defeat. And, more to the point, it was nothing to do with him. Except, what if something had happened to her? She was new to the city, didn't know its dangers, was way too trusting. Maybe he should keep trying. Purely for safety's sake.

By midnight, he found himself accidentally slouched in front of the security cameras that covered the main foyer. There was a monitor in his apartment, so he could check who was asking to see him. He'd dragged a chair over, watched, and waited, snacking on popcorn and bitterness. It wasn't a riveting show until the door opened and she tottered in, wearing a skirt so short it was a moral outrage, and heels so high they made her the Leaning Tower of Leah.

Helping her along, holding her hand, was Rick Machin. Looking way too smug and pleased with himself.

Chapter 14

Rob had stood up, dropped the popcorn, kicked the bowl so hard it flew to the other side of the room, smashing into the wall. It arced tiny yellow kernels through the air as it went, scattering them all over the carpet like golden hail. He kicked again, and the chair fell backwards, banging down to the floor, its leather back crunching into the popcorn. Other than the monitor, there was nothing left to kick, so he forced himself to calm down as much as his blood pressure would allow.

Damn. His mother must have finally convinced her to go on a date with Rick. He wasn't an idiot; he knew Dorothea liked Leah, saw her as some kind of redemption. Knew that she wanted to make him jealous, make him realise what he had to lose, as though he was a teenager again. Well, it looked like she'd won – she'd persuaded Leah to take Rick up on his offer. And it looked like Leah had enjoyed every single minute of it, if the giddy look on her face was anything to go by.

And can you blame her, he wondered, when you all but pimped her out yourself? He'd sat there, hungover at the dining table, feasting on his own pain, and told her in front of witnesses that it was time for her to move on. Told her, in that cold voice he'd put on to try and close her down, that it was time for her to find someone new. Okay, he'd been hurting, deep in the darkness that surrounded Meredith and her death, but he'd been so harsh. Rejected her, in front of his family, like the bastard he was capable of being.

Even then, she hadn't given up. She'd still tried to reach out. Still clearly believed that they could be friends, that she could help him.

In return, he'd spent the next week wallowing in work and self-pity, stomping on every olive branch she held out. He'd sent his own message, loud and clear: back off. He hadn't even thought about how that would make her feel; how much that might cost her on top of the recent wedding fiasco. Hadn't thought of anything but himself and his own peace of mind. He'd been blinkered and selfish and cruel.

So now it served him right if she was finally doing it. Finally backing off. He'd made his bed, and Rick got to lie in it.

He picked up the chair, righted it, and sat down, shell-shocked. Tried to calm down. Did some deep breathing that made him sound like a congested seal. Stamped on some stray popcorn, grinding it into the shagpile. Told himself this was a horrifically predictable he-man reaction. He'd come home determined to get Leah out of his life. All this was doing was giving him a helping hand, and if he could switch his testosterone levels down from Neanderthal, he might even welcome it.

What Leah does, he told himself, and who she does it with, is officially None Of Your Business. He couldn't have it both ways – push her away with one hand, and keep her crushed against him with the other. Much as he wanted to, that was too sick, too screwed up for even him to contemplate.

She was entitled to a night of fun. To a lifetime of fun. God knows he hadn't offered her any since she'd landed in Chicago; he'd been distant, cold, downright nasty. He'd taken the connection they'd shared in Scotland and buried it. Buried it, shovelled dirt over it, and covered it with concrete. And despite all that, Leah had stayed... Bright. Shiny. Optimistic.

She needed fun. Heck, she deserved it, was made for it. Plus it was true, Rick *was* a nice guy. Rob had known him for years; and even as a 110% heterosexual male, he could still see why chicks liked him. He'd seen Rick in action, and it was impressive. He was sharp, witty, good-looking. There was a reason Rick had his pick of the women he met, a reason he never seemed to come across a single girl who ever said no to him. Rick had earned his rep for being a player, for being the guy most likely to bag the unbaggable. He could make the Virgin Mary head for the condom machine if he was on form. Leah would be easy prey in comparison, especially after a few glasses of something boozy. Defences down, head swimming, those big amber eyes glazed...

It was that final thought that had him up, out of the door, and scurrying down the fire escape steps to the floor below. None Of His Business be damned. So what if his mother had been right, and he was jealous? So he was male. That didn't change anything long term. It didn't mean he wanted Leah in his life. It just meant he didn't want her in Rick's. Oh hell, he'd figure out what it meant later. Right then, he was concentrating on taking the steps three at a time, barefoot, and not landing on his ass.

He hadn't taken the elevator, realising he'd look like a stalker if he coincidentally appeared on her doorstep as she arrived there with another man. Almost as though he'd been doing something weird...like watch her on a security camera. He could imagine the scene, elevator doors pinging open to reveal the shambling mess he was at the moment — unshaven, baggy sweats, bits of popcorn stuck in his hair — just as a perfectly coiffed Rick Machin smooth-talked his way into her bedroom. No, far better to hide in the stairwell, peeping out of a tiny crack in the fire door, that was far less creepy. Right up there in the serial killer handbook.

And after what he'd just seen, he felt like a serial killer. And maybe he would be. He'd track down every man he ever saw Leah with and kill them. That, or sign up for some serious anger management classes.

Because even after Leah had shut the door behind her, even

after Rick had waved and left, he still felt tense and fuelled with adrenaline and misplaced anger. He was bouncing with it. All hyped up and nowhere to go.

Watching them laugh together, hold hands, kiss. Even without hearing them, it was overload. He'd rarely felt such rage flowing through him. His hands were shaking with it, and his breath was coming in short, ragged bursts. He was consumed with his own messed up fury.

He'd been stupid to bring Leah back to Chicago. Stupid to encourage her to see Rick. Stupid to come and watch them whisper sweet nothings in each other's ears. The list of stupid, it seemed, was never-ending, mixing up with anger in his brain to make a potent Screw You cocktail.

He kicked the fire door, hard. Doubled up in pain as he felt the bone of his bare big toe impact against the metal. Great, he thought, falling down onto the step, grimacing. Pain. Stupidity. Anger. Whirling around inside him, making him so crazy he tried to karate kick steel doors with bare feet. It was chasing away all his control, all his intellect, all his… guilt.

He realised he'd spent the last three hours thinking about nothing but Leah. He hadn't been thinking about Meredith at all. The name, usually an ever-present whisper in his mind, had been gone. Wiped out, no matter how temporarily. He sat on the cold stone step, rubbing a toe he thought might be broken, and frowning.

For the first time since her death, Meredith had been chased completely out of his mind. Even during sex, with a few notable recent exceptions, she was never far away. Now, he felt her absence. Felt the niche in his heart where he usually kept her, empty. She was gone; and even conjuring up the smell of her perfume didn't bring her all the way back like it usually did. He should feel guilty about it, he thought. But somehow, he couldn't manage even that. Couldn't even retreat to the harsh comfort of emotions he was familiar with; emotions he'd called home for a long time.

The guilt wouldn't come because, even now, sitting here like this, all he could think about was Leah. Leah and Rick; his mouth on her mouth, his hands sliding onto the curve of her butt, the way he made her laugh, so breathless and happy. About the way she'd giggled all the way back into her rooms.

About her lying there now, in bed. Just feet away from him, not even knowing he was back in Chicago. Thinking about her new lover.

Maybe she was naked. Maybe she was thinking about Rick Machin as she fell asleep. Maybe she was regretting sending him away, wishing she'd invited him in after all. Maybe she was imagining him there, doing things to her. Maybe...

No. He had to stop right there with the maybes, or he was going to kick down the door and do something they'd both regret and he could probably get arrested for. He couldn't see her right now. Couldn't risk the words that might come out of his mouth, not when his brain was this sweltering mass of anger and rage and confusion. He didn't understand anything about his feelings for Leah. He didn't understand if he wanted her to leave, or stay. He didn't understand if he wanted her friendship, or her hatred. But he did understand this: she was driving him insane, whether she meant to or not.

He limped back up the stairs, and back into a world of solitude and broken popcorn.

Chapter 15

Leah woke the next morning feeling every one of her 25 years. Which made a refreshing change from the other 40 or so she'd been borrowing from someone else the last two weeks.

She didn't know whether it was her date-that-wasn't-a-date, or simply the fact that she'd slept nightmare-free for the first time since she'd been in Chicago, but the fresh morning light striping its way across the bed fitted her mood perfectly. She reached out and pressed the remote control, waiting for the swoosh as the drapes opened. She would never, ever get fed up of that, she thought, blinking as winter sunshine flooded the room.

This morning, she decided, is the first morning of the rest of your life. Yes, Rob is still there, like an ache in your heart. Or a bunion on your toe. But life is for living, not for wasting. The irony wasn't lost on her that while she was busy trying to convince Rob of exactly that, she'd been allowing herself to slip into a slow depression, waiting for him to respond.

The obvious fact was he didn't want to respond. He was like a drowning man ignoring a hand reaching out to grab him. And if he was determined to end whatever mutant spark had developed between them, she could do no more about it. She certainly couldn't do any more waiting, or use up any more energy trying to figure out what was going on in his head - she had to get on with her own life, and simply say a prayer for his.

The date with Rick hadn't ended with fireworks or passion, despite his very best efforts. But Leah had lived most of her life without fireworks and passion, and it hadn't been so bad. She'd gained a friend, if not a lover. And who was to say that at some point down the line, say in a couple of decades or so, she wouldn't forget all about Rob Cavelli, and find someone new? Someone else who could make her pulse race with nothing more than a half-smile? Make her forget her own name just by kissing the soft skin of her shoulder?

Either she would or she wouldn't – but worrying about that, or worrying about Rob, would do nobody any good. It was time to start moving, and keep moving.

She had three apartment viewings lined up for the next day. Dorothea had paid her in cash, so she had the money to put down a deposit if she saw one she liked. And tomorrow evening, she had a meeting arranged with a potential client to discuss catering for a Ruby wedding anniversary. There was a lot to do, and none of it needed to involve any emotions other than hope and determination. She would be busy; she would be successful; she would be independent. She would make I'm Every Woman the soundtrack to her life.

Which just left today to enjoy the luxuries of Cavelli Tower. While she still lived there, and he was in New York. Because independence, she knew, was likely to come in the form of a one-bed studio so far outside the Loop she wouldn't even be able to see it.

Leah had planned to use the Tower's pool since she got here, but somehow between jet lag, parties and trauma, she'd never managed it. It was on the penthouse floor, and today was the day. She jumped out of bed and rooted around until she found the bikini she'd bought at the airport. It was red with white stripes, and she thought it made her look like a saucy sailor from an old seaside postcard. Even looking at it cheered her up. This was going to be a day of perfect displacement activities, she decided.

Of happy, busy solitude.

Within a few minutes, she was implementing stage one: the pool. She was in the water, pretending to be in the Olympic synchronised swimming team: head under, legs up, scissor kicking the air. She rotated back up, landed on her back with a splash. She spluttered out the water she'd swallowed and gasped for breath. The rich really did know how to live – she'd never been able to have this much fun in the municipal pool. Not without amusing the local teenagers, anyway.

"Crikey," she said out loud, shaking her hair and blinking her eyes, "that was a lot harder than it looks."

"Really?" came a voice, echoing slightly around the pool room. "Because it looks ridiculous. Mind if I join you?"

She kicked herself around until she faced the edge of the water, already knowing what she was going to see. Who she was going to see. And how he was likely to be dressed.

"Well it's your pool, do what you like," she said, swimming over to the side and pulling herself up and out into a sitting position. All the better to escape from.

Rob loomed above her, his body as lean and bronzed and perfect as ever. She tore her eyes away from his legs. They only led up to hips, and that could only lead to trouble. She started to wring her dripping pony tail out as a way of shielding her face. She didn't want him to see how surprised she was. How nervous she felt. How annoyed she felt that her day of simple pleasures had just got a lot more complicated.

"I thought you were in New York? Don't they have pools there?"

"Yes, but without the added bonus of scantily clad women disco dancing underwater. How are you, Leah?"

"That was called synchronised swimming, and I'll have you know it's a recognised Olympic sport. And I'm fine, thanks," she replied, trying very hard not to jump when his bare thigh brushed against hers. He was sitting down beside her, long legs dangling down into the water; wearing snug blue trunks and with a white towel slung around his shoulders. He was staring straight ahead, as though he felt awkward as well. If he did, she thought, it served him right. For behaving like a prick for weeks, and for not back-tracking out of the pool the minute he spotted her splashing upside down like an epileptic Shetland pony. That would have been the gentlemanly thing to do.

"You're fine? Is that true? Because I thought I might have upset you," he said, kicking small circles in the water with his feet, the movement making the muscle of his stomach clench and unclench in a way she didn't want to notice. She dragged her eyes away from his abs and saw that one of his big toes was swollen and purple, so bruised she could practically feel it throbbing.

"What happened to your toe?" she asked, pointing down into the water. "Did you drop your ego on it?"

"Very funny," he replied, glancing down at his own foot and frowning, like it reminded him of something he wanted to forget. "Long story. Are you going to answer my question?"

She paused, thought about it. Was she? Should she?

"Are you sure you really want me to?" she said. "And after two weeks of silence, do you think you even have a right to ask how I've been?"

"Probably not, but I'm asking anyway. So this is your chance to kick my ass, Leah, if that's what you want to do."

She did want to kick his ass…And she also wanted to stroke his ass. All at the same time. It was way too confusing for a day that had started so well. Why couldn't he have just stayed in New York for 24 more bloody hours and spared them both this?

"Right," she finally said. "If you insist.Today I'm fine, genuinely. But as for the rest of the time? No, not what you'd call brilliant. In fact, my thumbs almost fell off from texting you, phoning you, and emailing you. In the end I had to stop, Rob. Have you any idea how hard it is to find work in catering without thumbs?"

He half-smiled at the lame joke, and her heart juddered. She literally felt it bopping up and down, and thought it might flop out of her bikini and land shaking on the tiled floor. This is bloody ridiculous, she thought. Even when you're angry, he only has to smile to make you turn into a human jellyfish. Pathetic.

"You're doing it again," he said. "That thing you do when you're upset. Making light. Making me smile when it's the last thing I should be doing."

She blew out a long breath, her exasperation carrying into the air of the pool room.

"Well for goodness' sake, Rob, what else do you expect me to do? Open up a vein and bleed out into the pool because you ran away and hurt my feelings?"

She shook her head so hard water spun from her curls, like an angry mermaid. Her toes only just reached the water, or she'd have been tempted to kick up spray. Or to kick him.

"You had your reasons," she continued. "You did what you thought you had to do. Yes, it sucked. Yes, I think you're an idiot. But I've had enough drama to last me a lifetime, and in my own annoying way, I'm being honest. You deal with things by hiding in your Bat Cave, I deal with them by making light. I refuse to throw plates and scream, Rob, I refuse to feed into it."

She was angry, and hurt – but fighting to control both. Because a screaming match in a swimming pool would do nobody any good.

"Feed into what? What the *hell* are you talking about?" he said, his own tone deepening as hers had risen.

"Feed into your guilt! You're crippled with guilt about your wife and your baby. And I get that, Rob, I get that more than you can possibly imagine! I thought I could help you; I was wrong. You made yourself clear, and it hurt, a lot – is that what you want to hear? Do you want me to tell you how much it hurt, or how angry I can feel about it, or how sad?

"I'm all of those things, yes. But I'm not in critical condition, and I refuse to let you add me to the list of things to beat yourself up about. The list of reasons why you can't let yourself be happy. I'm looking at apartments tomorrow, I have work lined up, and

I'll be out of your hair as soon as I can. Then you can get on with the business of half-living your life again, without any interference from me."

"Good. That'll be for the best. Clean break," he said, his voice low, muted, so quiet she could hardly hear him over the sounds of the water sloshing gently against the sides of the pool. His fists were clenched, pummelling his own thighs, and every line of his body looked stretched out with tension. He refused to meet her gaze, and his mouth was set in a twisted line. He'd aged ten years in a matter of minutes.

She'd mentioned his wife and baby. She shouldn't have done that; Leah knew she shouldn't. For years after her mum and dad died, she couldn't bear for anyone else to talk about them. Even the most casual mention had felt like a punch in the stomach, piercing her careful self control. It was the same with him and his family, she knew.

But she wasn't perfect, and the anger had ridden her to the point where it just came out. Where it had to. She'd crossed a line that he wasn't ready to cross, and probably never would be. She reached out to touch him, brushed her fingers against the granite of his shoulder, over the bulk of his deltoid.

"I'm sorry, Rob," she said. "I'm sorry I lost my temper, I had no right to—"

"Don't give it a second thought," he replied, shrugging off her hand sharply. He couldn't bear for her touch him right now. Not when everything she'd said had left him so raw and wounded.

Her fingers curled away as though he'd slapped her, and her eyes looked haunted. He hardened himself to it, put a couple of inches between them. Something about this woman stripped him bare, exposed all his nerve endings, hit so many nails on the head at once it left him full of holes. And even now, feeling the anger that had flared up between them, feeling the shock that any mention of Meredith always brought, he wasn't immune to her touch. To the way she looked in that ridiculous bikini. To the feel of her skin on his, and the wordless promises it made: promises of comfort, and warmth, and intimacy. Promises he couldn't afford to hear. She wasn't his, would never be his.

"Let me know if you need any help moving out," he said, once he'd moved away, watching as her hand trailed in a sad arc to the floor. "Although I'm sure Rick will be on hand."

"Rick? What do you mean?" she asked, frowning in confusion at the sudden change of subject.

"I saw you with him, last night. Kissing him. So I know you mean it when you say you're well and truly ready to move on."

"And how did you see that? It's not as though you could have just been passing, is it?" she asked, honing straight in on the one question he didn't want to answer. He'd rather break the rest of his toes than tell her the truth. It was too humiliating.

"It doesn't matter how I came to see — are you denying that you kissed him?"

"No, I'm not denying it," she replied, her tone starting to fizz again. He'd forced her back into anger. Good. Anger he could do, better than anyone. If she was angry, he could keep her at arm's length. It was the empathy he couldn't deal with.

"I have nothing to hide, Rob. We kissed. I'd been on a date with him. A date you told me I should go on, shortly before you donned your Cloak of Invisibility. I didn't realise I was supposed to ask your permission before we did tongues."

Leah felt his whole body tense next to hers, and saw his knuckles whiten as he gripped the fabric of his towel. Oh God, she thought, there weren't even any tongues involved. But for some reason she needed to lash out. Make it clear he wasn't her boss, or her father, or her moral guardian.

"You're right," he said, still refusing to meet her eyes. "I did encourage you. And I was right to. I hope you'll be happy with your new boy toy."

Even as he said it, Rob cringed inside: what he'd just said was utterly ridiculous. Rick was the same age as him, and a

132

well-established legal mind. Hardly a boy toy by anyone's standards. But like so many things when he was around Leah, it just came out that way.

"God, you are so infuriating!" she said, scrambling to her feet, not caring if she was dripping on him.

"You've made it crystal bloody clear, Rob, that you don't want to have sex with me. You've made it just as clear you don't want to be friends with me. You won't discuss what you told me on New Year's Day, even though any idiot can see it's eating you alive. And now, after all that, you think you have the right to talk to me in that *disappointed* tone of voice? Like I've turned into the village bike because I dared to kiss another man, while you were off ignoring me? How dare you!"

Rob stood, unable to bear the sight of her bikini-clad body bouncing around above him while she yelled. He needed to concentrate on this, to have his mind switched on, but the jiggle-a-thon going on over his head was making it hard. Literally. Sometimes being a man really sucked.

"I don't even know what village bike means!" he yelled back, his own anger kicking in. He knew she didn't deserve it, but he welcomed it like an old friend – he wanted to feel rage and frustration and fury running through him. It was so much easier to deal with than the lust; than the affection; than the jealousy. It was the jealousy that really worried him – because to feel jealous, you had to give a damn.

"It means you think I'm a slut, Rob, to put it bluntly. Is that the case? Are you one of those men who's happy to jump into bed with a woman, then judge her for it afterwards?"

"Not a slut exactly, but —"

"But what, Rob? What? Because I can't figure it out. I care about you, I really do. But for some reason, that upsets you. And when I back off, that upsets you as well. You don't want me, but nobody else should have me either? Is that what you're saying?"

Her amber eyes were sparking with outrage, her blonde hair

shaking wetly around her face. She looked… perfect. Too perfect. He had no idea what he was trying to achieve here. The sight of her with Rick had completely thrown him; the sight of her here, this morning, in hardly any clothes, was only making it worse. And if he was confused, how the hell did he expect her to feel? Jeez. He needed to go and live in a shack in the Himalayas or something, he wasn't fit for normal human company.

"No. You're 100% entitled to your own life. To your own relationships. You should get out there, you should date, Rick or anyone else. What you and I had at Christmas was great, Leah, but let's face it, it was only a temporary distraction. It was sex, and nothing more. We should both be aiming higher than that. In fact, I'm seeing someone tonight. Who knows? Maybe she'll be the one."

She glared at him, eyes the size of saucers suddenly swimming with tears. She gulped, as though swallowing down her words, and Rob could see small tremors running through her body. Emotion. Anger. Or maybe she was just cold.

"Fantastic!" she said, her voice as icy as the goosebumps on her wet skin, rising to a shrill crescendo as she continued: "I'm thrilled for you – who is the lucky woman? Have we met?"

"No," he snapped back. "You haven't met, unless you served her hors d'oeuvres at the party!"

Right. Fine, thought Leah. That was her well and truly put in her place. She was a slut, a temporary distraction, and a servant. Why the hell had she ever thought she could be friends with this man?

"Staying in or going out?" she asked, hands on hips, lip the very definition of 'stiff' and 'upper'. Managing to drag an air of dignity around her despite the sopping bikini and shivering flesh.

"Staying in," he said, "in case I get lucky."

"Great. I'll cook you both something truly special, it's the least I can do – a special thank you from me. How about oysters, make sure the night goes with a swing? And I'll throw in a side order of arsenic for free!"

134

Chapter 16

Leah spent the rest of the day doing things she'd been putting off for far too long. Like emailing her friends, and finally having the dreaded conversation with Doug. They'd messaged each other for the last couple of weeks, but she hadn't felt ready to actually talk to him.

He apologised, and she told him it was okay. Because it was. The last few weeks had taught her something very important: what she'd felt when she caught Doug doing the dirty with Becky wasn't painful. It wasn't even close. In fact, it was a pale imitation of the way she was feeling right now, like catching a splinter in the thumb compared to having a stake driven through her heart.

"It was sex and nothing more." Rob had said. More than the snubs; more than the silences; more than the aggression, that's what had hurt her the most. She didn't quite understand why – it's not as though she expected to marry him and raise little Cavellis together. But somehow, it had stung, like an emotional bitch-slap. And, to top it all, tonight he had a date. Undoubtedly with someone skinny and appropriate and highly unlikely to be caught snivelling over a man who didn't want her.

God, she was a mess. And she only had herself to blame.

She dialled the next number on the Rebuilding Your Life list. Fred Larsson, slum landlord extraordinaire. Well, hopefully not, she thought, as she told him over the phone that she'd take the apartment he was offering sight unseen. Andersonville, the 'Swedish ghetto', as Marco had jokingly called it. She'd seen the neighbourhood on her journeys on the Red Line, and liked what she'd seen. There was a Farmer's Market, which would be useful, and a big gay scene, which would be comforting. If she never met a heterosexual man again, she'd be happy. From now on, she'd be a friend of the friend of Dorothy, and lock her libido in a cupboard where it belonged. It was only likely to get her into more trouble.

She glanced at her watch. It was almost 7pm. She'd left a message for Rob saying to expect dinner at 8. She was, after all, the kind of woman who served hors d'oeuvres at a party. He'd replied with his usual charm telling her not to be so stupid, he didn't expect her to wait on them. Them. Him and the mystery woman. Her response had been super-polite: "Tough titty. Payment in kind against the money I owe you."

So she'd been out to the fish market, and bought the oysters, which were chilling in the fridge downstairs. She'd keep it simple, lemon juice and ice. She'd baked a cake, in the shape of a love heart. And she'd bought a few props, which were now hanging on the door of her closet.

Was she really going to do this? Yeah, she was, she thought, pulling down the hanger and getting ready. Time to go out in style.

***

Rob was up in his apartment, wondering if there was any way he could get Amanda off his lap without using a Taser.

It was his own fault, he knew. Telling Leah he had a date was a big, fat lie, one he then had to back up with a real life woman. If he hadn't claimed he was on a promise, he could have been spending the night alone, getting drunk, watching the Cubs on TV. Instead he was here, wondering if he should be checking his glass for rohypnol.

Amanda had made it perfectly clear at the party on New Year's that she was interested, and in a parallel universe, he might well have taken her up on her offer. Now, he felt vaguely trapped beneath the elegant lines of her body. Like one of those gazelles being stalked by a lioness in wildlife documentaries. Except he was the gazelle, and he didn't much like the feeling.

On the one hand, he was thankful. It was Saturday night, she was gorgeous, she had to have had plans – all of which she had dropped to come round and have a fake date with him. On the other hand, she clearly didn't know it was fake, and had arrived with a loaded agenda. An agenda that involved getting him naked as soon as possible.

For some reason – well, a reason that began with 'L' and ended with 'h' – he wasn't interested. Amanda might be beautiful; she might know tricks in bed that would make a porn star blush, and she might be 100% available, but he knew he couldn't go through with it. Casual sex had been a regular part of his life for a long time now. Casual sex with women just like Amanda – sophisticated, stunning and single. It had suited him fine, until Leah came along and spoiled everything. Made him realise that not only was he bored with the shallow connections he made, but that the sex wasn't even that good. Not compared to what he'd experienced with her. All of which was scary shit, and part of why he lied.

He'd lied about having a date to make himself feel better, and to make her feel bad. Bad enough to drop all interest in being his friend; bad enough to hate him. Bad enough to walk out the door without a backward glance. And this, he thought, grimacing as Amanda nibbled on his ear-lobe, was the price he had to pay. She tried to slip a hand inside his shirt, and he held her wrist firmly to stop her. Jesus. Subtle, she wasn't – in fact he had the awful feeling she saw him as a challenge, and the more he resisted, the more determined she became. He looked up at her intent gaze; could so easily see her face morphing into that of a roaring lioness.

He heard the ping of the elevator doors, and the thought ran through his mind that he'd been saved by the bell. He stood up, holding Amanda around the waist and steadying her back onto her feet, ignoring the pout. He'd been pouted at by the best, and it really didn't bother him. Not as much as it would bother him for Leah to walk in on him being date-raped, anyway. Which was ironic, as the whole point had been to flaunt the fact that he had his own love life. One that didn't involve her. This was his chance to do that to perfection, but now it came to the crunch, it felt forced, empty. Cruel. Seeing him there with Amanda would be enough, he didn't have to rub it in by virtually having sex in front of her as well. Even he couldn't stoop quite that far. Plus he didn't know if he was even capable. The way things had been going, he could add erectile dysfunction to his list of woes.

"Coo-ee! Anyone home!" Leah shouted as she made her way through to the lounge area. She was doing something strange with her accent, something that made her sound like an extra from Oliver Twist, or the servants in Hollywood costume dramas. He heard the wheels of a trolley being pushed through, and steeled himself for her arrival, trying to look calm, in control, and utterly thrilled to be on a date with another woman.

It was a good plan, but it failed the minute she strutted into his line of vision, bending low to push her silly little trolley. Nothing, nothing at all, could have steeled him for the way she looked as she burst through that door in a blaze of comedy glory. She was dressed in the most outrageously slutty French maid's outfit he'd ever seen, complete with a frilly white apron and a minute black satin skirt that revealed lacy stocking tops and suspenders. Perched on top of curled blonde hair was a tiny white maid's cap, tendrils escaping around her face like golden cobwebs. Skyscraper stilettos meant that she tottered towards them, her décolletage wobbling as she moved, dangerously close to escaping a top so low-cut it almost hit her waist. He felt his jaw dropping, and suspected he'd never get it back up again without medical assistance.

She looked ridiculous. And gorgeous…And angry.

"Cor blimey guv'nor," she said, in that fake Cockney voice she never usually had, "don't you both look fine tonight – if you don't mind me saying so, sir, that shade of lipstick is just lovely on you!"

Rob realised belatedly that yes, his mouth, his neck, his cheeks – everything — was covered in Amanda's bright red lipstick. His hand went automatically up to wipe it away, but on cue his date giggled, and clasped hold of his fingers. Staking a claim he didn't want her to have.

Amanda didn't know Leah. Didn't know that she wasn't always like this; that the Hollywood version of sexy serving girl was purely for his benefit. A dig at him, and the things he'd said earlier. The way he'd reduced her to the hired help, insulted her and the part she played in his life. Hurt her feelings. Again.

Well, if she'd wanted revenge, she'd got it – he was incapable of speech, possibly of breathing. Even if he had been interested in Amanda, his desire would have wilted like a sun-starved flower the moment Leah walked in. He could never even conceive of another woman existing when she was standing there, looking like that.

"Now then, sir, milady, I'll just leave this here for you. Careful with those oysters, mind, slippery little buggers and no mistake! I'll be in my hovel below stairs if you need me at all, just ring the bell and I'll be right up – I'm at your service, Lord Cavelli, sir. Will that be all?"

Rob nodded curtly, not trusting himself to speak. There was simply no safe way to respond, not when he was simultaneously annoyed and aroused. She was bursting out of the stupid dress, and apparently he was still very male when it came to Leah. All she had to do to get him going was stand there looking like a wet dream, when his dinner date had left him cold despite her attempted tonsillectomy.

Leah glared at him, eyes shining, then dipped her knees into an actual real life curtsy. She turned to leave with a flounce, and the skirt bobbed up to reveal matching frilly white panties, inches of creamy flesh spilling out between their edges and the tops of her hose. He was fairly sure people in the next building must have heard him gulp.

The elevator doors pinged closed behind her, and he was dragged back to reality by Amanda, saying something dry about the British really going the extra mile in the name of service. Amanda. The woman he was supposed to be having a date with. She was running her fingers over his arm, sidling into him, her smile wide with anticipation. Anticipation of a something that he knew he couldn't do, even if he wanted to.

"Amanda," he said, pulling away from her, "I'm sorry, but there's been a change of plan."

***

Downstairs, one floor below, Leah was sobbing as she packed her bags. She'd slammed the door behind her, tugged the maid's cap out, clips still attached to her hair, and thrown it to the floor. Within minutes she had her suitcase on the bed and open, and was haphazardly throwing in everything she could lay her hands on: tops and jeans and underwear and moisturiser and ear-rings and iPods and toothbrush, all piled up on top of each other, like the Bad Girls Guide to Disastrous Packing.

Tears were streaming down her face, and she knew she must look like a demented panda. No mascara on the planet was water-proof enough to withstand that torrent. She was crying so hard she could barely breathe, forcing herself to gulp in tiny mouthfuls of air between sobs.

Way to go, Leah, she thought. Great plan. The plan to go in there and give as good as she'd been given. He'd belittled her, made her feel like nothing more than paid help who offered benefits on the side – and she was rubbing that back in his face with her whole routine It had sounded like a good idea at the time. She'd look gorgeous and sexy, make her point, and leave triumphant – with him salivating in the background. Show him she still had her spirit, that he hadn't broken her and never would.

Except... Except when it came down to it, that's not how it felt. She hadn't felt sexy, she'd felt desperate. She hadn't felt triumphant, she'd felt humiliated. And he had most definitely not been salivating – in fact he'd barely registered her presence, just stared at her, silent, covered in that woman's lippy. The same woman who'd been draped all over him at the New Year's party.

They'd obviously been getting down and dirty, and who could blame him? She was tall. Skinny. Stunning. Nothing at all like her. Not, for example, wearing fancy dress and flashing her knickers in an attempt to look hot. Oh God. It was so embarrassing. And painful – devastatingly painful, seeing him there, smattered in lipstick, holding her hand, obviously waiting for her to leave so they could pick up where they left off. She'd wanted to show she wasn't broken. And now she felt like she was shattered into a million tiny pieces. It had all been a lie: a stupid attempt at humour, at bravado, at provocation. And now she knew – she needed to leave. To sound the retreat, and lick her wounds, and one day find the will to live again.

She grabbed up her make-up bag, shoved it into her suitcase. Followed it with her trainers. Paused to sniff and swipe at her drenched eyes.

She was an idiot, on so many levels. To have come here at all, with him. To bloody Chicago, for Christ's sake, when all she knew was London. To think for a minute that she could help him. To assume that she could be his friend. To be so arrogant to imagine that she could reach him when his mother and his brother had failed. And to tell herself the biggest lie of all: that she could do all of that as just his friend, that she didn't want anything more. Seeing him there, covered in that skinny bitch, had proved one thing: she'd 100% deluded herself. Of course she wanted more. In fact she wanted everything. Everything he wasn't willing to give.

As she stood there playing Sally the Slutty Serving Girl, she'd realised something: her feelings for Rob Cavelli had gone way beyond friendship. Way beyond seeing him as someone she could help. Way beyond anything she'd ever experienced before – and into love. She loved him. She loved every ounce of him; she adored him and wanted him and cared for him in a way she'd never thought a human being was capable of.

Seeing him with another woman had brought it all collapsing in on her, like an avalanche of pain, an avalanche she was now trapped beneath. She was in love with a man she couldn't have. Rob was beyond her reach in every possible way, and there was no use kidding herself this could ever have anything but a miserable ending. One that involved her turning into one of those old ladies who live with cats and sleep on piles of old newspapers. Pining for Rob would be the equivalent of throwing her life away – she may as well have laid down in the snow on Christmas Eve, and given up.

She couldn't have him. She knew that, and it was killing her. But that didn't mean she had to stick around and watch someone else have him. If anyone had asked her two weeks ago, she'd have claimed she would be happy for Rob to find love in another woman's arms. Now, with the realisation of how she felt about him closing in around her, she knew she'd been lying. To herself and everyone else. She couldn't watch, couldn't be near. She had to leave this place, leave him, and never see him again. The North Pole wouldn't be far enough away; and she'd have to settle for a suburb a few miles down the road. Until she came up with a new plan. Salvaged what she could from this disaster and got away.

Even though her apartment wouldn't be ready until tomorrow, she had enough cash to stay in a motel for the night. As long as she wasn't fussy about sharing the en-suite with rats, or having luxuries like clean sheets. She didn't care: she'd rather spend the night with Norman Bates than stay here, imagining what was going on upstairs; imagining Rob with lipstick all over other, more intimate parts of his body.

She tried to slam the lid of the case shut. Predictably it was jammed open – hair straighteners poking out of one side. She shoved them in, preparing to jump up and sit on the case to try and close it. Breakages be damned – she needed out of here, quick.

She was perched halfway on when a hammering started at the door. Somebody wanted to get her attention, and they weren't bothering to use the bell. They were using fists, hard and insistent; so hard and insistent that the door might come off its hinges if she didn't open it.

She gulped. Knew it might be him. Probably was him, in fact. He was angry with her. Why? Maybe she'd messed up his date? Or embarrassed him in front of his guest? Spoiled his chances of getting laid? Oh lord. What should she do?

Leah jumped off the bed, and walked towards the door. She refused to look in the mirror on the way – it couldn't possibly tell her anything she wanted to know after twenty minutes of solid sobbing. Anyway, it didn't matter what she looked like. This would probably be the last time she ever saw Rob, and if she looked like the Creature from the Deep when she did it, tough.

She sniffed again, wiped the latest bout of tears from her cheek, and shouted: "Okay, okay! I'm coming!"

It sounded suspiciously like he'd started kicking the door now, which would never do. Not with that poorly toe of his. She turned the latch and pulled it open, keeping her distance in case he fell in. He did, mid-kick. She'd have found it comical if there'd been even an ounce of humour left in her poor battered heart.

"Oh please, feel free to come in!" she snapped, trying and failing to keep him out of the bedroom. He pushed past her, all arms and chest and gorgeousness. He'd dressed impeccably for his hot date: tailored black trousers that hugged the bones of his hips, emphasised the length of his thighs. A white shirt with a sheen of silk stretched perfectly over the muscle of his shoulders, open two buttons at the top to show a hint of that golden skin, the strong column of his neck. His hair was still slightly too long, and he'd obviously been shoving his fingers through it again, cornrowing it into unruly dark tufts.

143

Yeah, he looked sensational. He always bloody did, thought Leah, feeling her misery bleat like a caged animal in her soul.

"What are you doing?" he asked, after his blazing eyes took in the suitcase on the bed, hair straighteners still sticking out at an improbable angle, wires trailing forlornly to the floor.

"What does it look like?" she replied, crossing her arms over her chest defensively. There was way too much cleavage on show for this scenario. "I'm getting out of your hair, like I promised, and I'm going tonight. I'm sorry if I messed things up with your date. I'm sure she'll forgive you a slutty housemaid if you flex your pecs at her."

"Don't be so stupid!" he shouted, making her jump. Lord, he was furious. What on earth had she done to deserve this now, when all she'd seen earlier was total indifference? "She's gone. I sent her away. I couldn't let her stay after that little performance of yours."

"I don't see why not," Leah answered, backing up instinctively. "It's not like I meant anything by it. Just another one of my pathetic attempts at humour – you know, the ones you hate so much? Call her up, get her back for the night. Shag her senseless – I don't care, she's welcome to you!"

"Really?" he asked, edging closer towards her, fists clenched into tight balls, voice now lower, more controlled, somehow even more dangerous. His dark eyes were sparking gold, narrowed as he glared at her, taking a long step forward for every two of her ungainly hops back. "It didn't bother you, then, seeing me with Amanda? It didn't bother you so much you came straight down here and started packing, and from the look of your face, crying?"

"No!" she said, pouring her heart and soul into that one word in an attempt to convince him. It was hard to concentrate when he kept moving towards her, so big, so angry. She felt like she was trapped in a cage with a lion, minus the whip and the chair.

She took one more step backwards, staggering on the stilettos, and slammed into the wall. Her spine bounced as she retreated as far as she could without the assistance of a bulldozer.

"You can screw who you like, Rob, and you don't need an audience! I'm going, tonight, and you never need see me again. Why is that making you angry? Isn't that what you wanted, isn't that what all this has been leading up to? Getting rid of me? Hasn't that been the bloody aim of all of this? The silences, the insults? The sex party upstairs? You wanted to show me you weren't interested. Well you succeeded. Sorry I was so stupid it took a while. Now leave!"

He took that final step forward, knowing she had nowhere to go. Placed his hands either side of her face and leaned down and forward, his mouth inches away from hers. He pushed his body towards her, until she was trapped, squirming beneath his touch. She wriggled, trying to duck under his arms and away, but he grabbed her hands, pinning them by the wrists against the wall. Pinning them a bit too hard, so she could feel the pinch of her skin grinding against bone. She closed her eyes, squeezed tears away. She would not cry. She refused to cry. She'd done enough of that for a lifetime.

"Yes," he hissed, his lips brushing against her ear, "that's what I want. I never want to see you again. I never want to feel like this again, the way you make me feel, Leah...out of control... wanting you so much it hurts. I can't stand it!"

He thrust his hips forwards to touch hers, and her eyes popped open, wide, amber, shining with tears. He was hard, and big, and pushing himself against her. She made a little murmur as familiar sensations flooded through her body: tremors of excitement as she felt him move, a throb of need deep inside her; a quaver in her throat as she tried to swallow.

"You want me?" she asked, her voice as small as her eyes were large. He nodded tersely, swapping his hands so he used only one to trap her wrists back against the wall, softening his grip slightly. He used his free hand to trail blazing fingers down her side, roughly tugging the black satin of her top from the waistband of her skirt.

"Of course I do," he said, reaching up and in, tugging her breasts free of her bra, holding an already swollen nipple so tight it felt

145

like it might explode. It hurt, and yet it didn't: and she wanted more. He leaned down, kissed her neck, nipped at the soft skin until she yelped.

"I want you every time I see you," he said, moving on to the other nipple, fingers harsh, that same combination of pleasure and pain. "I look at you, and I need you. I need this. And I hate you for it."

With the last few words, he ground himself into her, and she spread her legs slightly, going up on tiptoe in her heels, desperate to feel the rigid length of him against her. She was already wet, knew she could never say no. No matter how rough, no matter how angry, she wanted him. Needed him. Her body betrayed her, and she pushed back, riding on the hard flesh that strained against her.

She should push him away. Knee him in the groin. Scream bloody murder. But she couldn't. And not only because of the way her body was responding – but because he'd finally admitted the way she made him feel. The way they made each other feel. After all the silences, the forced indifference, he'd acknowledged it.

"Well I'm here," she muttered, eyes flickering backwards as he hit the sweet spot, the spot that would, if he carried on thrusting, bring her to orgasm. "If you want me, take me."

A low grunt escaped him, and he dropped her wrists, moving his hands lower down her body, over her back, holding her tight against him, crushing her so hard all the breath whooshed out of her. He took hold of the hem of the skirt, pulling it up and his hips back, so his fingers had better access. He tore at her white panties, half pulling, half ripping, until she was completely exposed, her most private parts on show while she was still dressed. Breath heavy, leaning against the wall, nipples sore, something akin to shame flaring a blush across her skin. Behaving like the slut she'd never been, and loving every second of it.

Her eyes met Rob's, and what she saw there called out to her: a need so raw, so primitive, it over-rode every other thought. This was physical, biological, animal. She felt it too, felt it echoed in the pulse beating through her body, in the moist heat between her legs as they waited for his touch, in the trembling of her thighs as they spread for him.

His gaze was serious, harsh, his eyes pinning her eyes the way his body pinned her body. She felt his hands on her thighs, gripping the flesh at the top of her stockings. Felt one hand move upwards, and a finger entering her. It was fast, and not gentle, and yet she was so ready. Ready for more. She thrust against his hand, letting him feel her need, letting him know what she wanted. What she needed. Him, all of him, inside her.

"Jesus," he muttered, his finger moving in and out in a steady rhythm, his thumb trailing a searing circle on the sensitive nub at the heart of her. "You're so wet..."

His breath was ragged, tearing out of him as he looked at her face, saw those astonishing amber eyes wide open and glazed with passion. He'd fought for so long to stay away from her, from this. To stay distant, stay safe. But it was always there, always just beneath the surface, this desperate need, roaring to be met.

He kissed her, hard, crushing her lips, invading her mouth with his tongue, biting and searching, angry with himself and angry with her and angry with the whole damn world. His fingers probed lower, moving and stroking and bringing her to the very edge of oblivion. He felt it in her breath when she came: a tight catch in her throat, a gasp that had nowhere to go, a body that went liquid. He caught her around the waist as he felt her legs slacken, stopped her falling to the floor as she climaxed, the hot, damp flesh of her clamping tighter and tighter around the two fingers he'd now thrust inside her.

Her face fell forward onto his shoulder, and her whole body was trembling. She was wet, and soft, and vulnerable. Dizzy with sated lust, all barriers down. Now. Now was when he had to have her. He fumbled with his zip, freed the now agonising erection from his pants. He grasped her beneath the thighs, fingers digging into that delicate flesh so hard he knew he'd leave marks, and pulled her higher.

She looked up, shocked, as he tugged her parted legs around him, resting them on his hips, her face now level with his. A moment of surprise, then a half smile as she realised what he was doing. She crossed her feet behind his back, tightening the grip of her legs around him, resting her butt against his interlaced hands. She leaned her shoulders against the wall, undid the buttons of her top, offering him the tips of her exposed breasts. God, she was wanton. A goddess. A whore and an angel all wrapped up in one sex-drenched package. He could practically feel the heat coming from her sex as she writhed around, trying to angle herself onto his erect cock.

He plunged himself inside her, slamming his hips up and outwards, using his strength to pull her down to meet him. He knew he was big, and knew he could hurt her, but just didn't care. All he cared about was slamming his flesh into hers, hammering into that sweet, moist home, burying his shaft to its hilt in Leah, and the blessed oblivion of her body.

He leaned forward, steadying his rhythm, and sucked one of her rosy nipples into his mouth, biting and sucking until she screamed with pleasure.

"Oh God, Rob, yes!" she shouted, her hands tangled in his hair, pulling his face closer to her breasts, all the time keeping up a relentless bucking thrust of her hips. He responded, banged into her even harder, feeling his face engulfed by the curves of her bosoms. She raked her fingernails into his shoulders, and he could feel the blood flow even through his shirt. He upped the pace again, as fast and as hard as he could, all the time sucking on the tight ridged bud of her nipple, until he felt the first ripples of orgasm start to tear through her.

She screamed his name, threw her head back, and he felt her tighten around his cock like a gloved hand, wrapping it in searing hot silk as waves of pleasure rode her body, and in turn him.

It was too much, too erotic to withstand, the feel of this beautiful woman coming all over him: coming so hard it felt like he was screwing her without even moving. One final push, as deep inside her as he could get, so deep he thought he'd never come out, and he climaxed, crying her name, more pleasure than he'd ever known spasming through his whole body. It felt like every part of him was shuddering to that orgasm: he felt it everywhere, in his chest, his eyes, the sudden weakening of his legs. It ripped through him until he lost himself completely to it.

When it finally subsided, and the shakes were measuring only a few points on the Richter scale, he looked at her. Legs still wrapped tight around his waist even as he softened inside her, arms clutched around his neck, hair wild around her face. Breasts exposed, nipples sore and red from his less than gentle touch. Bite marks on her neck where he'd sucked at her flesh. Eyes dazed from orgasm, but sore from crying, her lids puffy and red, make-up striping her skin. Mouth bruised and swollen from kisses that came from anger instead of affection. The dark imprints of his fingers in the flesh of her thighs. God, had he really done all of that?

He walked over to the bed, Leah still wrapped around him like a little monkey, using one hand to support her and one to sweep the suitcase away. It slid to the floor, spilling its contents over the carpet.

He laid her down, and managed to disentangle himself long enough to lie next to her, cradling her head onto his chest and wrapping her body up in his arms. He pushed tangled blonde hair away from her face, ran fingers over the deep red marks he'd made on her creamy skin. Pulled the covers up over them, not wanting to see her torn panties, or the manhandled lace of her bra. They were vivid reminders of what he'd just done, and he was ashamed enough already. It hadn't been rape – God knows she was more than willing – but it hadn't been kind either. It had been rough, selfish, driven by rage and desire. He sighed, kissed the top of her head as she snuggled closer to him, as though she knew what he was thinking.

"It's okay," she said, nestling into his chest. "It was nothing I didn't want just as much as you did."

He had wanted it. Needed it. He'd lost control in a way he never had before, and it was unforgivable. To him, at least. And now, he didn't know what the hell to do about it. This woman lying in his arms, so small, so soft, so giving, could bring him to his knees. Make him forget himself. Make him forget Meredith. Make him forget their baby. Make him forget everything in the entire world apart from her. After weeks of fighting to keep his distance, to keep his sanity, nothing felt more right than to have lost it all again.

It terrified him, but not as much as the words she muttered next, face splayed against his still heaving chest.

"I love you, Rob," she said, oh so quiet, squeezing the grip of her fingers into his sides, wrapping her thigh over his. "I know you can't love me back, but I had to say it. Even if it's only this once, I had to say it. Stay with me tonight, Rob, just tonight. Then tomorrow, I'll be gone, and if it's what you want, I'll be gone forever."

He felt the trickle of her tears through his shirt, touching his chest like they were made of acid.

He clenched his owns eyes tight, feeling the emotion well up within him. She asked for so little, and gave so much – one night. Yes, he could give her one night. But how would he ever let her go again?

Chapter 17

Leah was choking. She tried to breathe, but every inhalation she sucked in filled her nostrils and lungs with bitter smoke. She coughed, held her hand over her mouth, fell to the floor. Tumbling, tumbling to the ground, wanting to scream for help but having no voice left, no air to use. Crawling across the floor, nose close to the smoke-stinking carpet. Heading for the fire escape, reaching out for the door, for safety.

She had to get there, despite the paralysis gripping her lungs, constricting her throat, stinging her eyes. She had to open it, throw back that door and let the fumes out, let the cool night air in, fill the room with life-saving oxygen. Inch by agonising inch she crawled, gasping for breath, until she reached it. She stretched up, grasped the hot metal in her hands, tried to twist the handle as her skin burned. It wouldn't turn. It was locked. Their escape was blocked. She had no energy left, nothing more to give. She'd failed. They were going to die, to die, to die...

"Leah! Wake up, Leah!"

She felt cool hands on her face, strong arms around her body. The sensation of soft carpet beneath her knees.

"Leah, it's me, it's Rob. Come on now, baby, you're safe with me."

The hands stroked her face; the arms held her tight against a firm chest, smooth skin over ridged muscle. She laid her head flat

151

against it, inhaled: fresh, clean air, and the smell of him. Of Rob. Of the man she loved.

It was only a nightmare. A nightmare, but a lot worse than usual. Her pulse was still thundering even though she was awake, and she was soaked in cold sweat.

Leah clung onto Rob, burying her face into his body, gulping in the breath her mind had been depriving her of for the last few minutes. She felt the familiar trembling flood through her body like a tsunami, the dryness tickling the back of her throat, the hollow feeling in her heart as she relived her father's final minutes. At least the way she'd always imagined them.

Then she cried, the way she always did in the aftermath. Cried for them and their final suffering; for herself and the fact that she missed them so much. For her guilt, and the way she blamed herself for them even being there. This time, she cried for other things too. For her failed attempt to replace the security of her family with the security of a life with Doug. For her failed attempt to outrun her unhappiness by fleeing to Chicago. Mainly, for her failed attempt to not fall in love with Rob Cavelli. Because she knew that loving him would mark her for the rest of her days, just like her parents' death had. It would claim some part of her that nobody else could ever reach. A scar that would never fade.

Throughout the sobs, Rob just held her close, rocking her gently. Stroking her hair, murmuring reassurances into her ear, whispering Italian endearments she didn't even fully understand. He picked her up, carried her back to the bed, and surrounded her shivering body with his. She cried until she was probably dehydrated. Let it all out in a way she'd never done in front of another person, not even Doug in all the years they'd shared the same bed. Eventually, the sobs subsided, and she let herself slowly, slowly relax. Her breathing returned to a slow, regular rhythm, and she felt as calm as she was ever likely to in the aftermath of one of her nightmares.

"Now, are you going to tell me what that was all about?" Rob asked, tilting her head up so he could look at her. "I woke up to find you crawling across the floor, choking, and trying to reach the door."

Rob stroked her poor, battered face. He saw the way her eyes were thick and swollen from a double dose of weeping; mascara was crusted around the edges, charcoal lines criss-crossed over her cheeks. Despite it all, she still had the most beautiful eyes he'd ever seen, those amber orbs gazing up at him, filled with pain and torment. Pain and torment that must have been there before, but he'd never noticed. Because he too damn busy being a selfish ass, consumed by his own problems. All this time, she'd tried to reach out, to show him she understood his guilt and his loss – when there was clearly a lot of pain going on in her own life.

She nodded, and her eyes glimmered again. She blinked tight, and he saw the effort she was making not to start crying. He kissed her forehead lightly, trying to encourage her without pressurising her. Heaven knows he hated that himself. If she wanted to talk, she would. If not, he'd understand.

"My parents," she said, voice still small and choked with emotion. "They died when I was eighteen. The night I turned eighteen, in fact. I wanted a party, so I asked them to bugger off for the weekend. They were great, my mum and dad. I was an only child and they always wanted to make me happy. So they did as I asked, and they went away."

"What happened?" he said gently, rubbing her arm. She was cold. Despite the fact that the apartment was warm, and that she'd spent several minutes crawling across the floor and screaming, she was cold.

"I lost my virginity, bully for me, and they lost their lives. Because of me. There was a fire at the hotel they stayed in, and the owner had painted over the fire escape locks. They found my father's body at the foot of the fire door, like he was reaching out for it. Mum never even made it out of bed. The owner was prosecuted, but that didn't bring them back. I was still on my own, technically an adult, in that big house all on my own. Knowing it wasn't only the owner's fault, it was mine as well – it was only because I was a stupid teenager hell-bent on becoming a grown up that they were even in that hotel. If I'd just gone to Tuscany with them to celebrate like they'd wanted, they'd still be alive today."

Her voice was bitter as she recited the story, angry, older than he'd ever heard it. Filled with a pain and self-hatred that he recognised instantly – because it identically mirrored his own. And despite that, despite knowing exactly where that tone came from and the depth of the feelings that inspired it, he had to say what he said next.

"It wasn't your fault, Leah. You can't blame yourself."

He felt her body twitch against his, as she issued a humourless laugh.

"And how many times have you been told that, Rob? I have no idea what happened to your wife and your baby, but Marco certainly thinks it was an accident. How many times have you been told not to blame yourself, that it wasn't your fault? And in all those times, have you ever managed to believe it?"

He tensed, the way he always did at the mention of their deaths. Felt his heart rate slow down, almost to the point where he thought it might stop. Sometimes, he'd wished it would. But she was right – guilty as charged. He'd heard it countless times, and it never made a jot of difference. No matter how many times the universe said it wasn't his fault, in his heart it always would be, just like Leah would always blame herself for a dodgy hotelier skimping on the fire code. She was as broken as he was; she just did a better job of hiding it.

Now he did at least know why she had been so insistent that she could understand him, understand his pain. He'd thought her naive, now he knew different. Because yes, she did understand. Better than anyone else in his life ever could.

He took a deep breath, stared up at the ceiling, dragging all his calm together until he could speak, put at least some of it into

154

words. Time to be brave, Rob, he thought. Time to discuss the one thing you've avoided discussing for years, instead of choosing to let it fester and grow like an emotional cancer inside you.

"My wife was called Meredith," he said. "The baby didn't have a name, although we'd always thought maybe Paolo for a boy, and Gabriella for a girl. It was a girl, it turned out. Gabriella Dorothea Cavelli, if she'd survived. If she'd even been born."

Leah stayed still and silent in his arms, and for that he was grateful. If she'd so much as moved, or whispered, or touched his face in sympathy, he couldn't have gone on. He nodded again, as much to himself as anyone else.

"Meredith was only eight weeks pregnant. She'd found out that day, and I can only imagine how excited she was about telling me. Waiting for me to come home from work. She'd told me she had a surprise, but I was working late. As usual. Made her wait, as usual. Days later, when I was going through some of her stuff in the bedroom, I found the pregnancy test she'd used, wrapped up in Christmas paper. Silly stuff with reindeers on it, and a big ribbon. She obviously meant to give it to me as a gift; a gift she knew I wanted.

"But I didn't come home. Despite the fact that it was Christmas Eve, and my beautiful wife was waiting for me, pregnant, filled with expectation, I didn't come home. I'm sure Dorothea's told you I'm a workaholic. These days, they blame the fact that I'm not right in the brain. They think it's all part of the grief, and to some extent that's true. But I was the same before, even when I had Meredith. She was the love of my life, Leah, and still I chose work over her – not just that day, but most of them. I lost track of the number of times I cancelled dates, missed dinners, left her at home on her own. All so I could work. I was a terrible husband, and she still loved me. Maybe she thought having the baby would change all that, and maybe it would. Or maybe I'd have been just as bad a father, I'll never know.

"On the night she was going to tell me, I was still in the office at eight. Despite the fact that she called me, told me she had this fantastic Christmas present for me. At which point it crossed my mind that I hadn't bought her a damn thing. Or my mom, or Marco. Hadn't even bothered to get Felicia to buy stuff for me. Typical selfish ass. Well, I felt bad then – when she mentioned her gift for me. I knew there was this necklace she wanted, that she'd hinted about. I'd even asked the jeweller to set it aside – but then completely forgot to pick it up. So you know what I did, Leah? I told her, on the phone on Christmas Eve, to drag her ass down to Miracle Mile and visit the jeweller. That he had a special something tucked away for her. And while she was there, would she mind picking up a bit of bling for Dorothea too, maybe some cuff links for Marco? Just like that, I asked my wife to go out in the freezing cold, in one of the worst blizzards we'd seen for years, and buy her own Christmas gift. Romantic, huh?"

Leah stayed quiet, but he felt her small hand creep into his, wrapping her fingers around his palm and squeezing gently. He nuzzled her hair, smelled her shampoo, tried to strengthen himself for the next part of his story. Because she deserved to hear it all, this woman who shared so openly and so willingly, who had done nothing but reach out to him since they'd met. She deserved the truth of exactly why he could never love her in return. Of why he wasn't capable.

"The snow was terrible. Ice everywhere. She was waiting at a stop light when a drunk driver shot through the intersection. He hit the driver side of the jeep before she had a chance to dodge him, and then two other cars coming from opposite directions ploughed into the mess. It was carnage, I saw the photos afterwards. Four vehicles were wrecked, but only one person died. Or, as they found when they did the autopsy, two. My beautiful Meredith, and our baby. Our Gabriella. They both died, because of me being a self-obsessed asshole who had to stay in work for an extra couple hours. Who couldn't even be bothered getting his own wife a Christmas present. Because of me."

156

His voice broke on the last word, and he felt tears stinging the backs of his eyes. Tears. He hadn't actually cried for years; he thought his tear ducts had dried up from over-use. After those initial months, a riot of booze and breakdowns, he'd stopped crying, stopped doing anything other than work. And here it was again, fresh as a daisy, stabbing away at him. He didn't even try to fight it, just let the tears roll, slow and fat, from the corners of his eyes.

Leah moved against him, shuffled her body upwards. She leaned down, kissed his face. Kissed the tears away, kissed his lips, kissed his eyelids. Kissed the tip of his nose.

"I can't tell you it's not your fault and have you believe me, Rob," she said, caressing his cheeks, stroking his hair. "Just like you can't tell me it's not my fault my parents died. We're obviously as stubborn as each other. But I am so sorry for your pain, Rob. And for them, for Meredith and Gabriella and everything you should have shared together. You were all cheated of a future that could have been golden.

"You won't believe me if I say again that it's not your fault. That if anyone is to blame, it's the idiot who drove drunk at Christmas. But I can tell you one thing – we have to try and keep on living, we have to try and manage the guilt and live our lives. I love you, Rob. With all my heart. And nothing you can tell me about your past, nothing you say or do, will stop me loving you. It's love. It's bigger than all of that."

He opened his eyes, met the amber pupils, and opened his mouth to reply. She laid a soft finger over his lips, made a quiet shushing noise and smiled. Tears fell from her face to his, merging with his own. Bittersweet, precious tears, blending together, the liquid expression of their mutual pain.

"I know, Rob. You don't need to say it. I know you don't love me; it doesn't matter. I still love you. And I'm still leaving today. Otherwise, you and I are going to play these games with each other forever. You with Amanda, me with Rick, or whoever comes along and plays that role. Hurting each other with sex. Hurting each other without sex. Constantly dancing round the fact that we're in pain. We both deserve better than that, Rob, and until we're apart, we won't break the cycle. So I shall take my broken heart, sweet man, and try to heal it. But remember this, when you're busy hating yourself – a woman called Leah Harvey once loved you. Loved you completely."

He reached up, cradled that lovely face in his palms, and wondered if it was possible to die of a broken heart. Because it certainly felt like it. She was right, she was doing the right thing, but the thought of her leaving... It was hurting him in ways he thought he was beyond hurting.

"I wish I could love you back, Leah," he said, pulling her face towards his for the barest of kisses. "I wish I could. But when I buried Meredith and Gabriella, I buried my heart with them."

Chapter 18

The next month of Leah's life passed in a blur of chaos and change. Good as her word, she'd moved out of Cavelli Tower that day. Rob had helped her pack properly, even managing to get the hair straighteners in, and driven her to the new apartment.

Neither of them was happy, but they had at last found some kind of peace through their honesty.

She'd said her goodbyes to Marco, to Dorothea, even to Artie the concierge. Goodbye to that phase of her life: the most thrilling, the most joyous, and the most painful time she'd ever experienced.

Her new home was a tiny bedsit studio in a quaint turn-of-the-century building. Quaint if you liked rickety stairs and antiquated plumbing, at least. It was above a coffee shop, and she could see the steamed up windows blinking with neon as they drove up and parked.

Rob had stood there in the middle of it, looming so large he took up the whole space, looking around with a distinct lack of enthusiasm as Leah hustled and bustled and tidied away her meagre belongings. Trying to hold it together. Wishing he would stay. Wishing he would go.

"Are you sure about this?" he asked, gesturing around him with outspread arms, almost touching both walls as he did it.

"Yes, I am. I like Andersonville," she said firmly. "And this place

159

isn't as small as it looks. It's only because you're so big. Once you're gone and I have the space to myself, I'll have room to move."

He raised his eyebrows, as they both registered that her statement could apply to life in general as much as her new home.

"You're absolutely right," he said. "And it's time for me to go. Good luck, Leah, and... thank you."

She nodded, reaching out to touch her fingertips to his, not trusting herself to do any more. Not trusting herself to speak in case she begged him to stay; not trusting herself to hold him in case she couldn't let him go. In case she shackled him to the bedposts and kept him forever.

He stared at her, then nodded. Like he knew how hard this was for her, understood the turmoil raging through her mind. He let his fingers stay joined to hers for one more heartbeat, then turned and left.

Leaving Leah with a half empty suitcase, no hot water, and a shattered heart.

Four weeks later, she'd managed to fix the first two. A bit of unpacking and a call to the landlord was all that had taken.

The third was still very much a work in progress, and proving more elusive. On that first day, she'd done nothing but cry. Huddled in her new bed, in her new life, grieving for the man who'd just walked through the door. Eventually, after hours of sobbing, she'd ventured downstairs to the cafe – wrapped in seven layers of clothing, eyes swollen, hair sodden with tears. She'd needed coffee, and they'd given it to her – along with cake, and company, and kindness.

Since then, she'd not contacted Rob at all, and banned herself from the evil temptation called google. The only way she was going to get through this was by making a clean break. Snapping the bone and hoping it healed straight – if it healed at all.

What Rob was up to was none of her business. She even banned Dorothea and Marco from telling her on their visits, despite Dorothea's not-so-subtle attempts to get her to open up.

Marco had loved the place; Dorothea had been predictably snotty, looking around as though she might get her clothes dirty just being there. Both had brought housewarming gifts – six packs of beer from Marco, hothouse orchids from Mrs C – which had been unexpected and moving. Her and Rob might have been a lost cause, but she'd gained their friendship, their sense of family.

Both of them, predictably enough, had wanted to talk about one thing and one thing only: Rob. And her. And what had happened between them.

Leah had stayed firm, refusing to be drawn out on the subject. It was private, and there was nothing they could do to help. Nothing they could do to fix it, no matter how hard they tried. She had to move on, had to try and heal the gaping hole in her heart. Having Marco banging on about Rob's all-consuming black-cloud mood wasn't going to help with that. Neither was hearing Dorothea sigh in worry about his eighteen hour working days, and his drinking. She couldn't afford to feel sorry for Rob, no matter how down he was. How depressed he was. And he wouldn't thank them for trying to pull her back into his world, when he'd only just managed to get her out of it. No, she had to think of herself now, and get on with her own life.

Marco had grimaced when she told him not-so-politely to shut up; but he'd done as requested – and obviously against his better judgement. He still thought that some miracle could occur. That if he – and she – tried hard enough, that Rob would 'come to his goddamn senses'. That with enough thinking, and enough effort, it could all end the way it should. As if.

Dorothea had been just as bad.

"But darling," she'd said, holding Leah's hand, "I was so hopeful. I thought you were going to fix him. You seemed so magical. I really believed you could bring my son back to life."

"Well I couldn't," Leah replied, her smile brittle. "I tried, but I couldn't. And what happens now is up to us, Dorothea – I know you mean well, but you have to let this go. Like I've had to let him

161

go. I won't survive this if you keep trying to drag me back in."

Dorothea had nodded, clenching back tears of her own, and let the matter drop. Leah knew it had taken a lot of effort, and was grateful for it.

That, and the support she'd shown for her burgeoning career. The one bright spot in an otherwise testing life. She had several juicy clients lined up, and had managed to snag a regular contract with the cafe downstairs, doing catering for their outside functions. She'd made friends – all of them gay men – and had even been out dancing. She had herbs in a box near the window, waiting until it was warm enough to go outside into the sunshine that she was told would emerge before too long. She even had an arrangement with her next door neighbour where she borrowed her Golden Retriever a couple of times a week to go for runs in the park. It was as much as she could hope for right now, and she was clinging to it desperately.

She was busy, had only had a couple of the nightmares since she moved in, and had cut the Rob-induced crying jags down to a maximum of one a day. They usually happened late at night, tucked up alone in the bed she pulled down from the wall every evening, when she couldn't quite stop her mind from drifting, from remembering, from torturing. From that stupid girl part of her brain that told her everything would be okay: that love would conquer all. That Rob would turn up one day and declare his love. That they'd get married and have babies and all would be well in their world. It was a fairytale, and she clamped down on it whenever it started to appear. If she gave in, if she allowed herself to indulge for even a few minutes, the pain of the aftermath was horrendous. Way too high a price to pay for a couple of moments of daydreaming.

That, she told herself firmly, would pass. The key was to keep moving forward. To stay busy. To maintain such a high level of physical and mental absorption that there was no way he could creep into her thoughts.

All of which, she knew, was great for her work ethic – but left her half alive. She'd been in her new apartment for a month, she realised, looking at the calendar pinned up on the wall over the sink. An anniversary, an achievement. She'd lived alone for a whole month, without burning the place down, flooding the building, even losing her keys. Life was looking up. It was the first time she'd lived alone since her parents died and it felt, well, terrible. But she'd done it. And she would continue to do it – because really, what was the option? There was no alternative, she knew that. Sometimes pain is simply too strong to avoid. You have to let it roll over you, cope the best you can, and look forward to that day – that glorious, fictional day – when you wake up and it's finally gone.

It was nearing the end of February, and the grey Chicago skies were starting to be evicted by pale blue swathes, streaked with hopeful gold. A promise of things to come. Today, she decided as she idly flicked through her post, she would celebrate. Even if it was only with a hazelnut latte from the deli, or baking herself some fresh cookies, or buying herself some flowers. She'd do something positive, something good. Walk the dog. See friends. Go to a movie. Refuse to cry. A celebration of surviving the first – and please God the worst – month of life without Rob.

She put the junk mail aside, amazed at how quickly she'd ended up on American sales lists as well as British ones, and focused on the one official looking letter. Brown manila, her name neatly typed in a see-through window. Those, she knew, were rarely good letters. She had a bad feeling about that letter, was reluctant to even open it. Today was supposed to be about celebration, and along comes this nasty, dingy envelope, looking all threatening and bureaucratic. Yuk. Doug had always dealt with official stuff back home, and even thinking of that fact made her feel doubly pathetic.

She paused, bit her lip nervously. There was a blurred ink stamp on the outside with a set of initials, but she had no idea what the acronym stood for, and couldn't even read it properly. Looked like there was only one way to find out...

She tore open the envelope, cursing as she made a tiny paper cut in the bend of her finger, and pulled the sheet out. She unfolded it, moved nearer to the window for better light, and read. And read again. And again. Over and over, until she was sure she had it right, that the words on the page meant what they thought they meant.

They did. She was being kicked out. Her work visa was being revoked, and she had twenty eight days in which to leave the country. Because of 'irregularities' that had come to light about her application. And if she didn't leave, she'd be subject to a fine, arrest, and deportation. Possibly, she expected it to say in the small print, with her head on a stake and poisonous blow darts aimed at her bottom. At least they offered to pay her airfare home, which was lucky, as she had about twenty two dollars in her checking account.

Leah sat down before she fell. She read the letter again. She breathed deeply, shouted 'clear!', and restarted her heart with an imaginary defibrillator. No. Still felt stunned. How could this be happening? She'd filled in all the forms Marco had given her. He'd checked them over, assured her that his contact at the Immigration Department would rubber stamp them. That she'd be fine to stay, to work, for at least a year. How could it have all gone so wrong, just now, when she was finally starting to find her feet? Finally starting to see some light creeping in at the end of the tunnel?

She read the letter once more, feeling the heaviness of it settle in her stomach like one of Popeye's anchors. It was there in black and white, and no matter how many times she read it, that wasn't going to change.

It was over. The American dream was over. All of her work, all of her effort, all of her planning was for nothing. It was all wasted.

Leah stood up, walked slowly and carefully, back to the calendar she'd been looking at earlier. Sunlight streaked in through the window, slanting across the elaborate love heart design of February's page. Valentine's Day. Hah. Work meetings were scrawled in, potential clients, dates of events. Signifiers of the fact that she was starting to turn her sorry little life around. Meetings that would have to be cancelled. Clients she'd have to let down. Food orders she'd have to stop. Shit and double shit. She traced her finger over the appointments, still feeling the shock of disbelief, the letter from Immigration now scrumpled up in her clenched fist.

She'd moved in four weeks ago. And now she had four weeks in which to leave. Four weeks in which to pack her whole new life into yet another suitcase, and head for home. Wherever that was. London? Hampshire, where she'd grown up? There was nobody left in either of those places, not really. She was alone now. Truly alone. And it was terrifying.

She grabbed the felt tip pen that dangled by the calendar on a string, blue-tacked to the tiles. Doodled a skull and crossbones on March 17. D Day. D for deportation. Four weeks to sort this monumental mess out. Should she call Marco, ask for his help? But how could she? After she'd rejected his pleas to help him with Rob? After she'd made it clear that she wanted to stand on her own two feet? She couldn't just go running back to him, tail between her legs. He'd already done so much, and he had his own cross to bear – his brother.

Leah stared again at the calendar, with its scribbled notes and jotted reminders. Lifted the pages up, looked back at January, and its pictures of snowmen singing Auld Lang's Syne, let the dates filter through her brain. Something was niggling at the back of her mind as she looked at the circled dates, the landmarks of her life. Yes, she'd been here for a month now. But something wasn't right. She was missing something. Something important. She'd kept herself so busy, she'd lost track of something she usually paid attention to.

She realised what it was, leaned against the bright yellow paint of the kitchen wall, and slid to the floor. She sat in a heap, wrapped her arms around her knees, and felt a shiver take hold of her despite the layers of woolly jumpers she was wearing.

Her period. She was missing her period. It wasn't marked on

the calendar because it hadn't happened – and normally, she was regular as clockwork.

She was alone, facing deportation, and possibly pregnant. It was going to take more than coffee and cookies to fix this.

Chapter 19

Two days later, there was no 'possible' about it. She'd trudged to the drug store in her snow boots, fighting off mild embarrassment as she handed over a fistful of dollars in return for a pregnancy testing kit. Gone home, drank coffee until she was ready to burst, then peed on the stick. Looked on in absolute horror as the pink line appeared. Read the instructions again. Read them a fifth time. Finally accepted what she was seeing – she was pregnant.

That last time, with Rob. That brutal, desperate mating; up against the wall in Cavelli Tower. Their passion and fury and desire driving all common sense from their minds. The thought of stopping for a condom hadn't even occurred to either of them. In Scotland, they'd been careful. Sane. In Chicago, they'd lost control – and gained a baby. Jesus. What a mess. How would she tell him? On the phone? By email? She could just imagine it: "Hi Rob, how are you? Just thought I'd let you know I'm having your child. Love and kisses, Leah." Maybe she could add some smiley faces to take the edge off the shock?

Maybe, she thought, she shouldn't tell him at all. Maybe that deportation notice had come at just the right time. Maybe it wasn't the disaster she thought it had been at first. She could just go: disappear off into the night. Her air fare was paid and, well, she'd figure out the rest when she got back to the UK. There was a welfare state. She could get help. There'd be free health care for sure, which was a huge bonus. She'd need that... she'd need pre-natal tests, and check ups, and blood tests. And a hospital to have it in. And mammoth amounts of pain killers. And she was definitely planning on having this baby, she realised.

At first, with the shock of it still settling in, she'd tried to weigh up the pros and cons. Tried to be sensible. She was too young. Too poor. Too useless. She couldn't even look after herself properly, never mind a baby – what did she have to offer a child? She didn't need to have it. There were alternatives.

And yet now, with the dust settling and her brain starting to look forward, she realised there weren't any alternatives. Not for her, not now. She might be young. She might be poor. But she could love – she could do that well. She would have this baby, their baby, and she would love it. Even if she couldn't buy it a posh pram and designer romper suits, she could give it love and security and comfort. It was part of her, and part of Rob, and there was no way she could ever do anything to harm it. Even the thought of it left her swamped with tears, her own arms wrapped around her tummy, protectively.

No, she would go ahead. There really was no doubt. The issue now was whether she did it alone – or whether she told Rob he was going to be a father. As he'd made no effort to get in touch with her for the last month, it was fairly clear that he was sticking to his guns on the whole no relationship front. He didn't want her. Didn't love her. Really, nothing had changed – and it didn't seem fair to tell him about a baby, forcing him to be honourable, do the right thing. Be part of a woman's life when he seemed to want to do nothing more than to stay out of it.

She should stay quiet. Go home. That way he could pretend she'd never existed – and she could get on with being a mother.

The decision felt right, and yet wrong. Wrong to keep it from him. Wrong to deprive him of the chance to have a child at last. Wrong to deprive the child of the chance to know his or her father, never mind all of the financial privileges being a Cavelli would bring. She just didn't know. Neither option felt good. In fact, it all felt bad. And she felt a bit sick, too, as well as exhausted. Mental stress, pregnancy, or possibly a lovely, stomach-churning blend of the two.

As her brain was starting to ache, and she was giving some serious thought to doing a spreadsheet on the pros and cons of both routes, there was a knock on the door.

Assuming it was Wanda, her neighbour, or Todd from the coffee shop, she staggered over, feeling a wave of nausea hit her. Yay, she thought. Party time. She was wearing her traditional three layers of clothing, hadn't brushed her hair in two days, and had been too cold to get in the shower that morning. She probably looked as great as she felt.

She pulled open the door, a half-hearted smile fixed on her face. Even that faded when she saw who was waiting on the other side: Rob. A dozen emotions swamped her at once: shock, horror, and underneath it all, relief. Relief at simply seeing his face again, at smelling his aftershave, at the thought of simply throwing herself into his arms, telling him all, and seeking refuge in his strength. Giving up the battle of staying independent, and making these difficult decisions all on her own.

"Hi," she said lamely, completely uncertain as to how to react. He stood in the doorframe, his shoulders blocking the light from the hallway, a half frown marring his face. He looked serious; older. Worried. She wanted to reach out and hold him; to stroke his hair and kiss his cheekbones, and tell him he was having a baby.

"Hi," he said, the frown deepening as he took in her dishevelled state. "Can I come in?"

She nodded, mumbled an apology, and moved out of the way. He looked on as she wandered absently over to the kitchen, and started to fill her kettle with water. He watched her fumbling with the plug, rummaging through cupboards, stubbing her toe on the fridge as she took out the milk. Typical English reaction, he thought – reaching for the tea.

She didn't look well, he thought, frowning. Her hair was wilder than usual; her clothes made her look like a bag lady, and she was pale. Distracted, with none of her usual perky charm. All of which made him glad he'd come – but tore at his heart as well.

"Um... how have you been?" she asked, as she robotically swished a tea bag around a mug, handing it to him even though he never drank the stuff.

"Fine," he replied, the brown of his eyes flickering across her tired features. Leah could tell he was concerned, and don't supposed she blamed him. God, she thought, I must look awful. The man of my dreams turns up, the father of my baby, and I look like death and can't even formulate a sentence. So much for telling him everything. Maybe I should draw a diagram instead.

The silence stretched into minutes, neither of them knowing what to say. This, thought Rob, was not one of his better ideas –resolving to say his piece and, and get the hell out of Dodge.

"I know, Leah," said Rob, "and I've come to see if I can help."

Leah gulped, felt a slurp of tea run attractively down her chin. He knew, she thought? How did he know? She hadn't told another living soul – there was no way he could know, unless he had spies in the drugstore, or was having her trash can searched. She felt a panic attack rising, along with the now-normal nausea, and put her mug down as a precautionary measure. Best not to add third degree burns to the carnage.

"What do you mean, you know? How could you know?" she stuttered.

A flicker of impatience crossed his face, like he couldn't quite believe how dense she was being.

"Marco told me, obviously,"

"Marco? How the hell does he know?" she replied, flooded with confusion. What the hell was happening? She was the only person who knew about the baby, and suddenly the whole Cavelli clan seemed to be involved. She'd been considering telling him, but now the decision seemed to have been taken from her hands, she felt shaky, uncertain, like the ground was shifting beneath her feet.

"His contact at Immigration told him – how else do you think, as you haven't bothered letting us know?"

Leah paused, stared at him as the confusion started to clear. He didn't know about the baby. He was talking about the deportation. She'd made a huge assumption, because at the moment her brain could only focus on one thing – the baby. He didn't know, and that, she realised, came as a relief. Because the way he was looking at her – so tense, so disapproving – made her feel like a cornered animal. Like if she made one false move, he'd be in for the kill.

"Oh, that," she replied, walking to the sink to throw the tea away. She couldn't stomach it right now, and she really needed to not be meeting his eyes if she was going to pull this one off. "It's fine, don't worry about it."

"Don't worry about it?" he said incredulously. "You're getting kicked out, and your response is 'don't worry about it'? What the hell, Leah? I know how hard you've been working. I know how many clients you've been seeing. I know how—"

"You seem to know everything, Rob – how clever of you. But as we've not been in contact for the last month, I assumed you didn't want anything to do with me, never mind regular reports on my progress. I guess your brother and mother must have been submitting them instead – or has Felicia been compiling memos for you? Project Leah: Update?"

She could see him bite back the anger, smother the words as they strained to leap from his lips. She'd got to know that face pretty well in recent times. It was his 'exasperated-by-the-lunatic-dwarf' face, and she hated it. It was rude, and patronising, and downright hurtful. It was the face that said he saw her as a liability; as a problem to be solved, as an inconvenience. Well, she'd had enough of that. There were some major changes coming in her life, and she could cope with it all by herself. She knew she could. She had to – there was no alternative. Because the thought of telling him now, of telling him about the baby, made her feel even more sick – she'd be stuck with that disappointed expression for the rest of her life.

"I didn't come here to fight with you Leah. I came to see if I could help."

"Very noble, as usual, Rob. And how exactly do you think you could help – not that I've asked you to?" No, she thought, you've done quite enough. You and your super-powered sperm.

"Well I've been discussing the situation with Marco. He might be able to sort it out, but he's not sure – there's not enough time. He says... he says the simplest way to fix this mess would be for you to get married to a US citizen."

"Bloody hell, Rob – you look like you're constipated! And what a stupid idea! It's not that simple, is it – what am I supposed to do, ask the bloke in the coffee shop to get hitched? Ask Rick to give up his life of sex and super models just so I can carry on living this ridiculous fantasy of making it here? Propose to the homeless guy who pushes trollies full of milk cartons through the park? What on earth are you thinking?"

"I'm thinking," he said, slowly and deliberately, rubbing the frown at the top of his nose as though he was trying to get rid of a headache, "that I could marry you. Purely for convenience. So you could stay, establish your career. We wouldn't even really need to see each other, and in a while, we could get divorced and never see each other again."

Leah fell down onto the sofa, looking up at his looming presence, the way he filled the whole room. God, how she thought she would have loved those words. Rob asking her to marry him. A fleeting fantasy of a wedding, of a life together, or raising their baby. Of rediscovering the Rob she'd known in Scotland.

Except that's all it was – a fantasy. That wasn't the man standing before her. He looked the same – glorious – but he was a different human being. One who was married only to his own grief.

"Wow. That's the most romantic thing I've ever heard," she

said, sarcastically, meeting his distressed gaze head on. "I feel quite dizzy with it all."

"Don't be so stupid, Leah – it's not romance you need, it's a visa! And I'm willing to do it – just say you will. It's my fault you're—"

"Stop right there, mister!" she said, interrupting him and earning a glare in return. "I don't want to hear the whole 'it's my fault you're here' speech. It's not your fault. It's not Doug's. It's not anybody's but mine. And as for what I need, I don't think you have a clue about that. You remember our last night together, Rob?"

"Of course I do," he said, his voice quiet and pained. He screwed up his eyes, and she wondered for a moment if he felt as tearful as she did. At least she had crazy hormones to blame it on.

"And do you remember what I told you?"

He nodded, lips clenched tightly, as though the thought upset him. It probably did, she knew.

"Look at me, Rob," she said, standing up and walking over to him. She reached up, stroked the side of his face. Felt it lean into her palm, like a puppy seeking comfort, then pull away. He looked at her, and she felt her heart cracking all over again.

"I told you I loved you, Rob. I still love you, despite all your best efforts. And now here you are, standing in my apartment, looking like you've just eaten your own liver, asking me to marry you. I can tell from that look that you will never be able to say that back to me. Maybe you'll never be able to say it to anyone. And I pity you for that, I really do.

"But I'm worth more than a fake marriage for the sake of a visa. I'm worth more than committing my life to a man who can never love me. I'm worth more than all of that. So thank you, Rob, for being willing to make such a sacrifice. But no – not unless there is any way you convince me I'm wrong about all of this."

She waited, barely able to breathe. It all came down to this one moment. Forget the visa, forget the marriage, forget the deportation. This was it: the moment where she would decide whether to tell him about the baby or not. The moment where she may

173

have to face up to life as a single mother. The way he reacted now would decide all of that.

He reached down, stroked stray tendrils of blonde hair away from her face. Traced the contours of her lips with the tips of his fingers. Looked long and hard into the glowing amber of her eyes. Gave her the only answer he felt capable of: "I'm sorry Leah. About everything. But you're right."

She placed her hand on his, stood up on tiptoes, and kissed him briefly, feeling the tears well up.

"I thought so. It's time for you to leave, Rob – and this time, don't come back."

Chapter 20

Rob looked around him, then back at the A-Z he held in his hands. Someone had told him the UK would be cold in autumn, so he was wearing black leather gloves. Ha. It was positively tropical compared to Chicago; a crisp, clear day, sunlight sparkling from frost, reddening leaves lining the sidewalks. Pretty.

He stared again at the map, trying to figure out exactly where he was. He'd been wandering around for ten minutes after getting off the Tube at St John's Wood. He could have used his driver – should have, in fact, bearing in mind he was lost – but he'd wanted the walk. Wanted to clear his head.

That, he realised, had been ambitious, as he was suffering from a severe case of jet lag and anxiety. A fantastic combination that was threatening to choke the breath out of him, and which had definitely retarded his map-reading ability.

He'd left Chicago yesterday, after his whole family ganged up on him. Marco, Dorothea, and even Melissa – Meredith's sister. They'd held an intervention, pinning him down in his apartment while he had nowhere to run. He'd felt it coming from Marco and his mom for months, in their silent disapproval, their not-so-subtle concern, the way they watched everything he did as though he were a nuclear bomb about to go mushroom cloud on them. But seeing Melissa, Meredith's sister? That had been a shock, one that hit him like a punch in the gut.

He hadn't seen her for four long years. Melissa, who he'd shame-fully cut out of his life at a time when they could both have supported each other. Melissa, who looked so much like Meredith that he couldn't bear to be in the same room as her. It just hurt too much. Every year she'd reached out to him, and every year he'd ignored her – worse than that, he'd had Felicia send her a standard, pre-signed Cavelli Inc. Christmas card. What an asshole.

Despite all of that, despite his rudeness and his selfish attitude, she'd come to Cavelli Tower. All the way from Miami, flying in from the Sunshine State just to kick his ass. Dorothea and Marco hadn't had to travel as far, but they certainly joined in with the ass kicking.

He couldn't say that he blamed them. It was his first night at home after a five-day bender that had started with the Thanksgiving turkey, and ended with him waking up on the floor of a jail cell, wearing lederhosen and a pair of bunny ears. Not a good look for a grown man. Not a straight one, at least.

Marco had bailed him out, and they'd driven home in silence. There'd been none of the ribbing he expected. None of the mockery his brother excelled at. Just a stern gaze, and barely a spare word.

He'd been deposited outside his room, and told to sleep it off, leaving Rob with a deep sense of shame and desperation. For once, he'd have welcomed Marco's incessant pushing; his persistent attempts to make him talk about Meredith. Make him talk about Leah. Make him talk about anything. Instead, it was like he'd given up. Given up on talking, given up on Rob.

Maybe he was right. Five days, for Christ's sake. Most of which he couldn't even remember. Anything could have happened, anything at all. He was lucky he'd only woken up with bunny ears and not a wedding ring; lord knows he had the money for a Vegas run. He could have been killed, or injured, or ended up in hospital with blood poisoning.

Instead, he'd ended up in the lock-up, where a kinder-hearted member of Chicago's finest had taken pity on him, throwing him in a cell to sober up before he did himself any damage. The last time he'd been in jail, it had been because of Leah. And, if he wanted to be bitter about it, this time was as well.

Hell, not just her. Everything. Everything that was wrong with his pathetic, screwed up life. Including the fact that she'd left, disappeared off the face of the planet without so much as a goodbye.

Marco and his mother had been furious with him, for giving up without a fight. For letting her go. For allowing her to get kicked out of the country.

"What the hell's wrong with you?" Marco had yelled at him, as angry as he'd ever seen him. "It's obvious you're in love with the woman – why didn't you just ask her to marry you?"

"I did," Rob had replied, looking his brother straight in the eye. "And she said no, okay?"

Not only had she said no, she'd done it in style. Left him broken, and bruised, and wondering if he'd just made the biggest mistake of his life. She hadn't contacted any of them ever again.

She'd disappeared off the face of the planet, or at least Chicago. All debts paid, no forwarding address, no way to trace her. She could be anywhere. New York. New Delhi. New Guinea. She was gone. She hadn't contested the deportation – just left, without a word to any of them. He'd spoken to the landlord, to the guys in the coffee shop, to her neighbours. None of them had a clue where she'd gone – or even when. She'd cancelled all arrangements she had with them, thanked them for their help, and pulled a major league vanishing act.

After that, Rob had retreated in on himself again. Never mentioned her name. Had Marco and his mother half demented with worry. They'd both seen it before – the way he'd behaved after Meredith died.

His eyes were lined with sleepless nights, his forehead creased with a permanent headache.

He'd been drinking heavily, working stupid hours, and locking himself in his rooms for the rest of the time. Even Dorothea threatening to spank him hadn't worked. He'd backed far away, and they'd started to fear he'd never come out the other side.

They were, Rob knew, right. For months he'd behaved like an ass. A self-destructive ass with a death wish he wasn't even honest enough to acknowledge. Leah living in Andersonville had been hard, but at least he'd been able to see her. Pick up the phone and hear her voice. Find an excuse to bump into her. Feed the sad addiction he suspected he'd have for the rest of his days. But life without her at all was impossible. It might have been what he claimed he wanted, but the reality of it was like a kick in the nuts with steel-toed boots.

It wasn't just that she'd gone, but that she'd gone without even saying goodbye. That despite the declarations of love, he'd meant so little to her in the end that she could abandon it all so easily, burn her bridges so brutally. Again, he couldn't blame her. Why wouldn't she? She'd done everything she could to make things right. And in return, he'd done everything he could to push her away – why was he so surprised when she took the hint?

After she'd gone, things got really bad. He was losing whole weekends to drinking, often alone, in bars where he knew nobody. Making the casual friends people made in such sad, dark corners of the city, where first names were the only names and buying a guy a drink was as intimate as it got. Until the week before, of course. Until the Thanksgiving incident, when he'd clearly made some very different friends. Friends who liked him enough to loan him lederhosen two sizes too small and pink bunny ears. That flashed. At least, he'd thought, sobering up in the jail cell, he still had both his lungs.

He'd woken up at home the next day still suffering from the hangover from hell, and faced by the daunting triumvirate. Marco, his mom, and Melissa. He'd choked when he'd seen her face; her kind brown eyes, her full lips. The caramel curls that were exactly the same as her sister's. The sweet smile the two had always shared.

178

The way she touched his hand as he shivered and shook, filled with grief and shame.

He couldn't refuse Melissa, no matter how much he wanted to. No matter how much he wanted to tell her to take a hike, to leave him alone with his booze and his misery. She was part of Meredith, part of his past. She shared DNA with the woman he'd once loved.

So when she sat on the edge of his bed, Marco and Dorothea hovering in the background, and took his hand, he couldn't resist her. And when she'd wiped away his tears, and calmed his trembling, he had to listen.

Had to listen when she told him: "Rob, it's time for you to move on with your life. You can't love a ghost forever. From what these guys tell me, Leah is an amazing woman. Someone you could make a life with. Don't you think that's what Meredith would have wanted?"

"I don't know, Melissa," he'd replied. "I don't know anything anymore."

"Well it is – I know it is, Rob. I know you loved Meredith. So did I, and we'll both always grieve for her. But you didn't die in that crash with them, no matter how many times since you might have wished you did."

He'd stared up at her in astonishment at that, amazed that he'd been so transparent. Melissa had simply smiled, and held his hand.

"And I ask you this now, Rob – if Leah was back in your life, would you still want that? Would you still be wishing it was all over?"

He turned the thought over in his mind, feeling the rawness of emotion stabbing and shearing and tearing holes in his already fragile soul. He held Melissa's hand tight, and looked into her eyes.

"No, if Leah was here, I wouldn't be wishing that."

"Why?" she asked, pushing him to put it into words. To make it real.

"Because," he said, "I love her."

God, he'd hated himself for so much right then: not just for his part in Meredith's death, but for abandoning Melissa afterwards. For letting Leah slip through his fingers. For losing himself in booze and self-pity for so long. For making a terrible situation so much worse. But all he could do now was try and make it right.

"But I don't know where she is," he'd said, his voice shaky. "I tried to find her when she first left, but I couldn't. Then I figured she didn't want to be found, and decided to leave her to it. Decided I'd messed her life up enough already."

"Well you didn't try hard enough, Rob Cavelli, did you?" Dorothea had piped in, waving a bony finger at him. "Good job I'm made of sterner stuff. She's in London. It wasn't that hard, and if you'd really wanted to find her instead of wallowing in self pity, you'd have hired a private investigator, like I did. I have the address, and you're booked on a flight to Heathrow tonight. Either you're on it, young man, or you're out of my life – for good."

He recognised the ultimatum for what it was: fraudulent. His mother would never disown him. Like she said, she was made of sterner stuff. But he also recognised it for something else – a second chance. A chance to redeem himself. To man up. To become the person Meredith would have wanted him to become, not some bunny-ear wearing barfly.

So now, here he was. Standing on St John's Wood High Street. Looking at chintzy chocolate shops and swish cafes and shop windows full of blingtastic clothes. Watching dark-haired women in glamorous outfits walking glamorous dogs. Searching for the corner that would lead to the street. The street where she lived.

He walked on, against the swell of shoppers, further towards the intersection he needed. Took the steps he needed to take, to the doorway of the bistro, with its fake French lettering on the hanging wooden sign.

It was tucked between a bookshop and a beauty salon, with wooden-framed windows and flowers in tubs outside the door, standing like sentries. It was just after lunch time, and he could see staff inside cleaning up, leaning on mop handles as they chatted, moving tables and chairs aside.

He paused for a moment; gathered his courage, fought of the very last vestiges of his hangover. God, he could kill for a drink right now.

He finally took the plunge, and walked in. His eyes scanned the room, wondering. Wondering if she was there. If she'd emerge from behind the bar with a towel over her shoulder, or if he'd hear her voice, her laugh. If she'd see him first and do a runner through the back door. If his mother was even right, and he wasn't on a wild goose chase. Maybe it was another Leah Harvey. Maybe he should just back out and leave.

A man walked up to him, tall, thin, sandy brown hair thinning on top. Attractive in that harmless looking way some women found appealing. He was wearing a black apron and a wary smile as he approached.

"Hi there – can I help you?" the man asked when he drew close. He smelled vaguely of red wine and garlic, the remnants of a lunchtime special wafting around the dining hall. It was all dark wood, candles in bottles, chalked up specials lined up at the bar. Atmospheric, nice. Scary as hell.

"Uh – yeah. I'm looking for Leah Harvey. Is she around?"

"And who would I say is calling?" the man asked as he wiped his hands on his apron. He stood back, looked Rob up and down appraisingly, taking in the American accent. The expensive cashmere coat. The soft leather gloves. The dark Italian eyes. The smile fell from his face as he realised who this visitor was.

"Rob Cavelli," Rob answered, staring back at him with equal hostility. Because a few things were starting to fall into place for him as well. Leah had never talked much about her previous life, but he knew enough to take an educated guess. To guess that this was the bistro she used to work in, and that this was Doug. Hide-the-sausage-Doug, in the not very substantial flesh. He felt his heart plunge to the soles of his boots. Were they back together?

Had she left him, left Chicago, to make up with Doug? He couldn't believe it. She'd said so many times that Doug didn't matter to her. She'd said so many times that she loved him, loved Rob... but maybe, not enough?

The man-he-now-knew-was-Doug straightened up, glanced over his shoulder as though checking for back up.

"She might not want to see you, Rob. She's not been well."

The tone in Doug's voice held a very clear subtext: because of you, you bastard. Rob was aware that several of the other staff had stopped what they were doing, were standing around, watching and listening. Staring at him with utter hostility. Looked like he'd just run foul of the Leah Harvey Fan Club, and he was first candidate for a tar and feathering. It was touching, in its own way – and he wasn't even remotely surprised. Why wouldn't they love her, and want to protect her? He did. It had just taken him a really long time to realise.

He reminded himself of that as he chose his next words.

"Look, Doug – you are Doug, right? – I've come a long way to see Leah. To make things up to her, if she'll let me. I don't know what she's told you, but I'm sure her description of me was nowhere near as bad as the reality. I treated her like crap, and I won't deny it. But I'm not the only one to have made mistakes, am I? Not the only one to have hurt Leah? We both have. And now I'm here, and I want nothing more than the chance to apologise, and hope she gives me one more chance. I love her, more than anything in the world. Maybe you do too, Doug – but doesn't she deserve the chance to decide for herself? If you guys are back together, and that's what she wants, then I'll wish you luck – but I intend to have the chance to hear that from Leah with my own ears."

Doug flushed slightly, his pale skin colouring easily at the mention of his own indiscretion. He pulled the tea towel from around his lean shoulders and rubbed his hands on it. His hands were dry and clean; it was obviously a nervous thing. He stared at Rob, as though weighing him up, trying to make the right decision.

The right decision for Leah. Rob tried to look as trustworthy as he could, tried not to look like a barbarian brute out to ravish the fairy princess. And the way the rest of the staff were glaring at him, there'd be mop handles in mysterious places if he played this wrong. He could feel their communal anger; they even seemed to take a step forward, like in a zombie film.

"Okay," said Doug eventually, after what felt like a lifetime of deliberating. "You get your chance, Rob Cavelli. She's up the stairs in the back, second door on the right. Knock before you go in – like I said, she's not well. And no, we're not back together – but if you upset her, even one little bit, you'll pay for it. You've done enough damage. Are we clear?"

It was hard for a man built like Doug to look threatening, especially against Rob, who was two inches taller and thirty pounds of muscle heavier. But he gave it his best shot, and Rob had to respect that.

He nodded gratefully, then walked up through the bar. Past the mop-wielding Leah-loving zombies. Up the stairs. Down the corridor. Second door on the right. He paused, took a deep breath. Had no idea what was going to happen next, but knew that the rest of his life depended on it.

He knocked, and waited. Wondered if they'd warned her somehow – phone, walkie talkie, zombie mind tricks – and if she'd even answer. If she'd tell him to go screw himself, or was already halfway out of the window. Knowing Leah, she'd get stuck, and he'd be confronted by her ass in the air as she tried to make the fire escape.

"Come in, I'm decent as I can be!" came her voice. God, her voice. How much he'd missed it. Her silly teasing, her inappropriate jokes, that crazy accent. He felt his knees weaken, like a great big girl.

He turned the handle, pushed the door. Walked in, knees still shaky. Everything shaky.

She was there, lying in a single bed tucked up against the wall of a small room. She was bundled under a pile of blankets, and the minute she saw him, she pulled them even closer up to her chin, hiding her whole body.

Her eyes widened so far they took up her whole face, and he heard an audible intake of breath. Her hair was longer than he remembered, like she hadn't cut it since January. It was so long, like Rapunzel, coiled over her shoulder and touching her lap. He wanted to run to her, to bury his face in it, to lose himself in the smell of her, the scent of her shampoo. To beg her forgiveness, and never leave her side again.

Instead, he kept his distance. She was staring at him with what he could only describe as horror, her fingers convulsively gripping the top of the blankets. Like she was afraid of him. Surely that couldn't be right? Yeah, that last time between them had been on the rough side, but she'd seemed okay with that. Unbothered by it. What had happened since then to make her so scared? He could see it in her eyes, in the taut stretch of skin around her mouth. In her silence.

"Leah," he said, taking one cautious step into the room, leaving the door open so as not to spook her even further. "How are you?"

It wasn't what he wanted to say. He wanted to apologise. To tell her he loved her, more than life itself. That he didn't want to go on without her. To ask her to come home with him, home to a new life that he'd make perfect for her, forever. But looking at her terrified eyes, the fine trembling in her shoulders, he knew he couldn't. Shouldn't.

"Um...how am I? I'm shocked, Rob. Very shocked. Why are you here?"

He shoved one hand into his pocket, and ran the other through his hair, the way he always did when he was stressed. Oh my, thought Leah, watching him. How tired he looks. How drained. There were lines on his forehead that weren't there a few months ago, shadows under his eyes that had appeared since she last saw him. Still magnificent, still heartbreakingly handsome, but subdued – anxious.

She was so surprised to see him, so lost in studying his face, she was finding it hard to think. To speak. She'd fantasised about this moment so many times over the last eight months. Imagined him walking through that door, taking her in his arms, telling her everything would be all right. Taking away the fear and the loneliness and the anxiety. Eventually, she'd trained herself out of it. She couldn't deal with the heart break, couldn't process the extra pain at a time when her body had so much else to be coping with. As the baby had grown inside her, she'd learned to love it – and learned to block thoughts of its father out of her mind as best as she could.

And now here he was, in the glorious flesh. Standing in her doorway again. Looking stressed again. On her territory; her baby's territory.

Did he know, she wondered? Was that why he was here? He'd somehow found out, and was doing the macho thing? The well-raised Italian boy thing? Was he here to make an honest woman out of her because he'd accidentally knocked up the waitress?

Because she didn't want that. If she'd wanted that, she'd have told him as soon as she realised she was pregnant. She knew Rob, knew his family – they would have stood by her. Been decent about it. Helped her out any way they could. That's part of why she'd left in the first place, so quickly. Before she had the chance to grow to the size of a house, like she was now. Before they'd had time to figure it out, to force her into accepting their support.

She'd called Doug. Figured he owed her something, at least. He'd come up trumps, meeting her at the airport, treating her like she was made of china. There was nothing left between them now, and they both knew that. Nothing apart from friendship, which she'd valued above all else. He'd given her the rooms above the bistro to call her own. He'd driven her to all her hospital appointments. Held her close when she sobbed after her scans; sobbed from the joy of seeing that baby growing inside her, sobbed with sadness at the fact that she was doing this alone. Without Rob. That, if she had her way, he'd never ever know about it. Never feel any sense of duty, any obligation to stand by her. If he didn't want her before she was carrying his child, she didn't want his pity. Didn't want a relationship based on a sense of responsibility.

And now, despite her best efforts, he was there. Larger than life and twice as gorgeous. Despite her swollen tummy, she felt something hormonal and basic respond to him deep inside. Felt her toes curl as she looked at his grim mouth; the darkness of his eyes. Felt her resolve weaken as she imagined how good it would be to lie in those strong arms again. To stop feeling so very lonely.

"Why are you here?" she repeated, realising that they'd spent the last few minutes simply gazing at each other. On cue, the baby kicked, hard and sharp beneath her ribs. He was big now. Almost baked, she'd joked to Doug, and ready to come out of the oven. Strong and healthy and letting her know he was there.

She winced, made a little cry, because it hurt. She was sore inside, and felt like she was carrying a beach ball between her legs. Pregnancy was simultaneously a beautiful and a horrifying experience.

He dashed over to her side, knelt beside the bed, the frown marring his brow showing her that he'd noticed. Of course he had. He noticed everything.

"What's wrong?" he asked, reaching out as if to touch her, pulling back when she shrank even further inside the covers, retreating from him in fear. "Doug said you weren't well – is it serious? What's going on, Leah?"

"No, no. Just a cold. I'm sure it'll be gone in a few days."

More like a week, she thought, knowing her due date like an old friend. A week until her baby would make his arrival on the scene. Her baby and Rob's. The baby he might not know about.

"Right," he said, his expression telling her he didn't believe it. He didn't push, and she was grateful. She wasn't up to an interrogation. Not from this man, who could still make her melt in places she'd forgotten existed. At least it seemed he had no idea about the baby. Doug might have sent him up here, but at least he'd covered for her, giving her a ready excuse.

"I'm here to tell you something," he said, still kneeling down beside her. "And to ask you something."

"Well, get on with it then," she replied. She knew she sounded snippy, but figured she'd earned it. She wanted him gone, back out of her life. Because before long she was going to need to get up out of this bed, and go to the loo. For the fifteenth time this afternoon. And she didn't want Rob around to see her floundering around looking like she'd eaten Wembley Stadium for breakfast.

"I'm here to tell you that I love you, Leah. That I love you with all my heart. That I've been an idiot. That I should never have let you go. That I need you to forgive me for being such a fool and letting you slip through my fingers."

Leah stared at him, mouth flapping open. Now that was not what she expected. Not in a million years. Could she believe it? Could it possibly be true? Could she simply be hallucinating, living out her dearest fantasy in her own addled mind? Maybe she was asleep...

"Is this real or am I imagining it?" she said, out loud, wondering if she should start pinching herself.

"It's real, sweetheart. As real as it gets. Please believe me - I love you. I loved you from the first moment you fell through my door in Scotland. I was spellbound from the first time I looked into your eyes. And like the fool I am, I spent every moment after that fighting it, fighting you—"

"Fighting your chance to be happy. Because you didn't think you deserved it."

Rob nodded, unable to reply. Completely in awe of her. Of course she understood. When hadn't she understood him? She'd known more about him after a few days than most people he'd hung around with for the whole of his life. She knew him, and she'd wanted him. She'd known everything about him – the good, the

187

bad and the ugly – and still she'd loved him. When he'd rejected her, when he'd hurt her, when he'd proposed both a marriage and a divorce in one sentence, she'd still loved him. Could he dare to hope that was still the case?

"Ok. Well, now you've told me something. And I don't know quite what to do with it just yet. What was it you wanted to ask?" she said, shifting uncomfortably under the blankets, her face squeezed with the effort of moving her body a few inches. He dearly wanted to know what was wrong with her, why she was in so much discomfort – but now wasn't the time to ask about that. Now was the time to ask something else entirely.

She looked on as he fished around in the pocket of his coat. Ran his fingers through his hair. Gave her the smile. That quirky, sideways half-smile that had always driven her wild.

"Well, at least I'm in the right position…" he said, offering her a small, square box. She stared at it, resting on the palm of his outstretched hand. Small. Square. Box. Surely he couldn't mean...

"Leah Harvey, would you do me the honour of becoming my wife?"

He did. He did mean that. The small square box contained an engagement ring, and Rob had just proposed. Down on two knees, to be precise, but it was the thought that counted. She was confused; stunned; nervous. There was so much at stake here. So much to gain, and so much to lose.

Even if he wasn't doing this for the sake of the baby, could she trust his motives? Could she trust him? She had someone else to think about now. A baby. A son. A son who needed her to make the right decisions for him, to raise him safe and secure, with or without a daddy.

Rob's hand was shaking, and he was gazing at her imploringly, waiting for her answer.

"Why now?" she asked. "What makes you think you deserve to be happy now?"

"I had a little help from my friends. And living without you these last few months has been hell, Leah. I wasn't coping well with life before, and I certainly wasn't coping after. The time we spent together showed me how life could be – so I shut it down. I didn't think I deserved it. But you know all about that. It took you leaving for me to realise how stupid I'd been. How I didn't want to live without you.

"I can't promise to be perfect. I can't promise to never be moody, or have moments when the guilt doesn't spill out again. But I can promise one thing – that I genuinely love you, with all my heart, all my soul. And that I will try so hard, so very very hard, to make you happy. To be the husband you need me to be."

She reached out, closed her hand over his, covering the box with both their fingers. He meant it, she knew. She could see it there, in those gold-flecked eyes. In the way he leaned towards her, so desperate to touch. Heard it in the passion of his words, the heat of his voice. Nobody could fake this, and no man on earth would be less likely to even try than Rob. Accepting that he loved her would have been one of the hardest things he'd ever done. No, she believed him. And, she thought as she gave herself a little pinch, she was definitely awake. It was happening, and it was scary, and it was wonderful.

He loved her. Rob loved her, and he wanted to marry her.

She smiled; a wide smile, a smile full of promise, full of secrets.

"I believe you, Rob," she said. "I really do. But it's not just husband material I'm looking for any more."

He frowned, confused. She was smiling. She looked happy. She hadn't slapped him. But she hadn't said yes either – and what did she mean by that last comment?

He was stammering out a question when she pulled back the covers, and inched herself slowly and laboriously to the edge of the bed.

"It's father material too, if you think you're up to the challenge. Give me a hand?"

Rob stood, staring down at her tummy, eyes wide in wonder.

Leah held up her hands, and he helped her to her feet. She was enormous, he thought. Surely about to pop. He tried to wrap his arms around her, found out he couldn't. She was just too round. Too big, too beautiful, too full – of his baby. Of a child that they could raise together, and love together, and watch grow together. He'd missed out on all of this, but he was determined not to miss one minute more.

"Did you know? When I turned up that day, offering you that romantic proposal of mine?"

"I did know. And I couldn't tell you, Rob, not after that. Not when you'd made it so clear you didn't want me. Maybe I'd have changed my mind after he was born – I never knew quite how I'd feel about that, whether I'd feel it was right to keep you in the dark. But right then, I needed to get away from you."

"I don't blame you, Leah. And you did a damn fine job of it. But now I'm here, and yeah, I'm up to it. More than I've ever been up to anything in my life. Give me the chance to make everything up to you. To you, and to our baby."

She grinned up at him, her amber eyes glistening.

"Well shut up and kiss me then," she said. "If you can find a way around Mr Bump."

He leaned down. And being Rob Cavelli - reindeer wholesaler, pirate white slaver, and the love of her life - he found a way.

Epilogue

The fire was crackling, small sparks periodically shooting off from the logs Rob had stacked it with. He gave it a jab with the poker, letting the ash settle before he returned to the sofa. To Leah. To his soon-to-be-wife.

It was Christmas Eve, and they were back in the cottage where it all began. This time, though, there was no wedding dress. And no misery. Just a very happy couple, and a stack of gifts under the mammoth pine tree that Morag had, as usual, decorated. This year, Leah had brought her own as well, adding in her own quirky touches to the tree, stocking the kitchen, bringing a sense of love and comfort to a place that had previously been barren and cold. To him, at least.

He climbed on top of her, pinning her easily beneath his body. She was even softer now, with a tiny bit extra around her tummy. Her baby blancmange, she called it, usually with a scowl. He didn't care. He loved it. Loved everything about her. Loved the fact that her body showed the marks of their baby; the tiny creature who had bound them even closer together. Their son, Luca. He couldn't wait for their wedding in the New Year, and was possibly even more excited about it than she was.

Leah wound her arms around his neck, tangling her fingers into the curl of his hair. Kissed him so well and so thoroughly that his eyes started to swim. There hadn't been too much hanky-panky in recent times for obvious reasons, and now he was like a teetotaller on his first drunken binge: he'd lost all his tolerance, and the slightest of touches sent him wild.

Of course, she loved that. Loved having him at her mercy. He ran his hand gently beneath her T-shirt, caressing her skin, sliding his fingers gently upwards. He felt her body arch towards him, knew what she wanted. For him to touch her there, on her breasts. He held off, teased her. Smiled down.

"Goes both ways, sweetheart..." he murmured, kissing her neck.

Just as he was busily working his mouth slightly lower, a piercing shriek screeched through the room. From the flashing baby monitor, which had been placed right next to his now-shattered ear drums. He jolted up, shaking his head to check if he'd gone deaf.

"Your son wants you," said Leah, rolling onto her side, grinning up at him. "And just like his daddy, what Luca wants, Luca gets."